HEAD CHEESE

HEAD CHEESE

JESS HAGEMANN

CINESTATE

CINESTATE.COM
@CINESTATEMENT
DALLAS, TX

"*Winesburg, Ohio* for the 4chan age, *Headcheese* isn't so much a novel as a living, gasping community, united by dismemberment, like phantom limbs holding hands across the world.

Headcheese isn't profoundly disturbing because its characters are fetishistic freaks, but because Jess Hagemann surgically inserts you so deep inside their reality that amputation begins to feel like a fundamental part of the human condition you've been missing out on your whole life.

Reading *Headcheese* is like realizing the chainsaw was the hero of *Texas Chain Saw Massacre* and that nothing brings us closer to our true selves than understanding what we'd cut away.

Jess Hagemann does for dismemberment what Ishmael did for whales—revealing the whole world inside the tiniest details."   —*Newsweek*

"A provocative and ingeniously assembled novel with enough debauched imagination—and perverse reality—to satisfy even the most morbidly curious reader. If this book was a Google search, you'd read it in incognito mode."   —**Katie Rife**, *A.V. Club*

Headcheese

Copyright © 2018 by Jess Hagemann

ISBN 9781946487117 *(paperback)*
ISBN 9781946487124 *(e-book)*

Library of Congress Control Number: 2018959029

Published by Cinestate
www.cinestate.com
Dallas, Texas

COVER ART & ILLUSTRATIONS **CHRIS PANATIER**

DESIGN & LAYOUT **ASHLEY DETMERING**
COPYEDITORS **PRESTON FASSEL**
DISTRIBUTOR **CONSORTIUM BOOK SALES & DISTRIBUTION**
ASSOCIATE PUBLISHER **JESSICA SAFAVIMEHR**
PRODUCER & PUBLISHER **DALLAS SONNIER**
AUTHOR **JESS HAGEMANN**

First Edition December 2018

Printed in the United States of America

For

LEO

NIC

&

TRICE

Players

(in alphabetical order by first name)

_____

THE GIRL. 11. F. Japanese. Somewhere in Asia. Not yet aware of her sexuality.

THE MOMMY. 40s. F. Filipino. Springfield, Illinois. Mother of four. Straight. Married. Quadruple amputee.

THE SKINWALKER. Ageless. Sexless. Raceless. Somewhere in the Arizona desert.

DR. C. 60s. M.

FR. W. 50s. M.

MR. B. 60s. M.

MR. D. 60s. M.

SR. J. 40s. F.

SR. M. 40s. F.

ANNA. 21. F. Thai. Washington, DC. Student. Pansexual. Single. Double wrist disarticulation and recipient of donor hands.

BARTHOLOMEW 'CAPTAIN HOOK' JORDAN. 30. M. Caucasian. Chicago, Illinois. Honorably discharged U.S. Army medic. Plastic explosives specialist at Mantid Labs. Director, Church. Straight. Single. Left transradial amputee.

CARLOS DELGADA. 17. M. Hispanic. Springfield, Illinois. Mentally handicapped.

DON. 53. M. Caucasian. Springfield, Illinois. Farmer, lay chaplain, and volunteer co-coordinator of a veterans' support group. Married to Petunia, but secretly gay. Right transtibial amputee.

ELIOT. 22. M. Caucasian. New York, New York. Paralegal. Gay. Dating Ira.

FOREST. 19. M. Mixed race. Washington, D.C.

Honorably discharged U.S. Marine. CNA at an adult daycare facility. Straight. Single. Right transhumeral amputee.

GEORGE MA'IITSOH. 76. M. Navajo. Chinle, Arizona. Retired professor of creative writing. Straight. Widower. Suffers from tinnitus.

HANNAH, AKA 'SANTA SANGRE.' 30s. F. Figment of Lorrie's imagination.

IRA. 33. M. Korean. New York, New York. Stockbroker. Gay. Dating Eliot.

JUNG-IL. 50s. Korean. Springfield, Illinois. Nail tech with a cocaine habit.

KAYLEE BRIGHT. Deceased. F. Gulf War veteran.

LORRIE. 32. F. Caucasian. Springfield, Illinois. Chief Communications Officer at a presidential museum. Heteroflexible. Single. Right transradial wannabe.

MONICA LIGHTFOOT. 42. F. Navajo. Chinle, Arizona. Toxic tort lawyer and tribal shaman. Bisexual. Single.

NATANJALI. 22. F. Indian. Travancore, India. Mother. Straight. Widow.

ODYSSEIA BAINES. 42. F. Caucasian. Copenhagen, Denmark. Sculptor. Lesbian. Single. Double transhumeral amputee.

PETUNIA. 53. F. Caucasian. Springfield, Illinois. Homemaker and baker. Straight. Married to Don.

QUINN. 30s. M. Caucasian. San Diego, California. Bartender. Straight. Single. Left transtibial amputee.

RALPH. 50s. M. Caucasian. Springfield, Illinois. Construction site manager. Gulf War veteran with PTSD.

SARAH. Deceased. F. Navajo. Wife of George.

TRICE KILLIAN. 39. M. African American. Washington, DC. Custom prosthetics team leader, U.S. State Department. Straight. Single.

UMI. 30. Female-to-male transgender. Washington, DC. Bouncer.

VICKI. 37. F. Caucasian. Washington, DC. Mother of Forest. Straight. Single.

WEEKO. 21. F. Navajo. Chinle, Arizona. Student and waitstaff, Two Spears Casino. Straight. Single.

XIOMARA DACE. 101. F. Hispanic. Springfield, Illinois. Retired. Widow.

YUPTAG. 60s. M. Japanese. Somewhere in Asia. Guru-warrior. Asexual.

ZED. 40s. M. Springfield, Illinois. Left transfemural amputee.

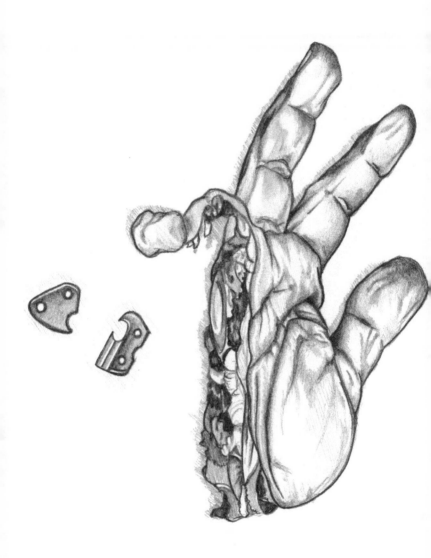

I don't have a sexual attraction towards amputees. But I have a horrible fascination with wanting to be amputated. Maybe I just want to be ruined.

I am interested in the removal. The after. And what happens to the limbs and the bodies.

I understand that for many people permanence is very important. But would anybody prefer the possibility of reversible amputations? I think it would be intense if rather than the changes being in my own control, they were in the control of a dominant partner. He could render me limbless and be the one to decide when I get those limbs back.

My fantasy is of being left with no limbs, incapable of independent movement, just a fucktoy to be picked up and used. Maybe with long-term wear of a bitchsuit my forearms and calves would atrophy so I wouldn't be able to use them at all, much like a quadruple amputee. I could live with that.

I also am strongly into the idea of having my penis removed, so I am unable to achieve release. I like the idea of it being a trophy for someone, particularly a dominant woman.

I want to be blind, too, and maybe deaf.

I believe I have had the symptoms of BIID since the age of 10, when I began to play the war amputee with my friends, and had recurrent dreams of losing my left leg in a fire or at the school playground. More recently I have been dreaming of being released from the hospital between two crutches, satisfied at finally being complete.

I fantasize about being kidnapped and having both hands and feet removed. I would have to live on all-fours like a pet.

I hate my arms and legs. I feel I shouldn't have been born with them. I think of myself as a torso until I look in the mirror. I would give up all my limbs if anyone wants them.

It is the first thing I think about when I wake up, all day long, and the last thing at night. I pretend when I'm driving that I'm using hand controls. I scoot around on my butt or walk on my knees when I am at home. I surf the Internet all the time for videos of amputees and fictional stories to read. I can't get away from it.

I have been this way all my life.

It's not like being suicidal, this compulsion **LORRIE** has. She doesn't want to actually die. Just, sometimes, Lorrie looks at her right arm and thinks it shouldn't be there. The arm seems an extra and very foreign appendage, like a super-sized skin tag, growing on account of nobody's fault but undesirable in its strangeness all the same.

When Lorrie considers her arm, it's with the dedicated intention of a teenage girl squeezing every last blackhead from the sides of her hormonally-afflicted nose. A gross thing, a bad thing—that must come out (or off) immediately—like a birthmark, or unfortunately large ears, or rather more unfortunately small breasts (the ears being easily hidden by long hair). Lorrie stares in the mirror at the parts of herself she hates, and imagines all the ways (short of magical thinking) to make them disappear. Her right arm and occasionally both bewildering feet.

From the massage chair at her favorite Korean nail salon, Lorrie leans forward to check on Jung-il's progress. Eight of Lorrie's nine toenails are a newly shiny shade of Pomegranate Punch, still wetly red and gleaming as the toe she cut off at thirteen.

It hadn't been with suicidal intention then, either, that Lorrie accidentally-not accidentally stepped directly down onto the sheet metal music box. She'd been curious, the way she was about girls that year (how much better they smelled, flicking their flower-scented hair behind them in long waves, than stupid, stinky, testosterone-charged boys).

She'd thought, *I wonder what it feels like* (to stick a finger inside yourself) (to be kissed) (to lie to your parents) (to become an amputee) (… *what?*) and like all those other experiments, this one had felt marvelously real, too; alive, authentic, part of (though not defining) her goddamn teenage identity. As the smooth copper plate bit into the baby-soft webbing between her pinky and fourth toes, it was a love bite of the highest order: reverential. Clean. Pure.

With that bright pain came a shuddering wave that peaked in the muscles near her newly-menstruating uterus, clenching and releasing in the most triumphant (read: first) orgasm little Lorrie had ever had. A truer sensation she'd never experienced, or since. Her first scout badge on the long and sometimes lethal road to amputee-dom.

In April 2002, **BARTHOLOMEW JORDAN** was a U.S. Army captain and platoon leader in charge of 18 recruits at Camp Victory in Baghdad, Iraq.

In May 2002, he was an honorably-discharged ex-Army captain, short two recruits and a healthy left forearm. The recruits he lost when their jeep triggered a buried IED. The arm he lost to a Sunni sniper with lucky aim. It was the single greatest moment of Captain Jordan's military career. Enough for a man with career military ambitions to retire on the spot and go to work for a Chicago-based start-up specializing in plastic explosives.

On paper, Mantid Labs produces C-4 for a wealthy demolition company. In reality, they work toward refining Sprängdeg m/46, a Swedish plastic explosive, by experimentally bonding pentaerythritol tetranitrate with the thermoplastic dibutyl phthalate. If successful, Mantid Labs will (secretly) own the only putty explosive with a higher detonation velocity than any other studied plastic, allowing for a sensitivity level identical to the Czech Semtex 1-A.[1]

On his first day at Mantid, Bartholomew Jordan flexes his fresh hook arm and is, well, hooked on the work. By day two, his co-creators have taken to calling him **CAPTAIN HOOK**. Bartholomew doesn't wear a red trench coat or a tri-corner hat, but he has the proud spine and broad shoulders of the captain he was, and the captain he is becoming.

---

[1] Used in commercial blasting, demolition, and in certain military applications; notoriously popular with Islamic militants.

TRICE KILLIAN rubs the tired from his eyes, and with a mighty yawn shuts down his system for the night. The 3D modeling software auto-saves then blinks out, momentarily leaving its inverse image on the suddenly black screen. The afterglow shows what looks like a robotic arm, a complex but exceedingly graceful web of fiberoptic filaments and cool blue metal. Hidden beneath a series of seamlessly articulating plates are nano-chips 1/12,000 the thickness of a human hair. These respond to body electricity as fluidly as motor neurons, facilitating every physical whim from a left hook that could, *Incredible Hulk*-style, smash concrete, to the gentlest caress of an infant's soft crown or a lover's lips. Scratch-resistant, waterproof, and easily dissembled for deep cleaning, one might even say the prosthesis is preferable to a real arm. It never gets cold or mosquito-bitten, has perfect handwriting, and executes every command flawlessly.

By the time Trice packs up his bag for the night and switches off his desk lamp—the only one still burning in the office—the image's afterglow has faded into top-level secrecy once more. On his way out, Trice flashes his badge at three different ID checkpoints, submits to routine fingerprint and retinal verification scans, slides his bag through an advanced X-ray machine that airports everywhere should have but don't (because this technology, too, is government-owned), then exits the Pentagon into a humid August evening.

At 32, **LORRIE** feels proud of the life she's created for herself. Single, yes, but in every other way successful: financially, spiritually, civically. Lorrie serves as Chief Communications Officer for a prestigious presidential museum that in addition to "making history come alive" for the children and parents of central Illinois, regularly hosts traveling exhibits on socially-responsible and timely topics. Celeb photographer Annie Liebovitz hung her under-appreciated landscape shots here (some of which showcased the president's hometown). An off-color version of the Body Worlds[2] installation displayed Siberian prisoners' preserved bodies and the traumas that killed them, which was relevant because four sitting U.S. presidents have been assassinated. Ever wonder what a bullet through the brain looks like on the inside? What poison does to the lining of a stomach? A half-severed penis, the teethmarks still evident? BodyHurts© had been a beautiful crime scene without the blood mucking up all the finer details.

Such exhibits are always interesting, and Lorrie loves writing the press releases that accompany a new exhibit opening, attending the preview with wealthy museum patrons to get a quote or two over a glass of state-funded sherry, nibbling locally-processed, small-batch cheeses, and skewering olives with more force than is necessary when pretending they are the corrupt (and corpulent) governor's yellow belly.

None of the temporary exhibits trump her favorite, however: a permanent exhibit tucked down a dark corridor in a rotunda, the walls of which are painted a lusty red. All the lighting comes from track-mounted spotlights aimed at fathead-wrapped press boards spaced evenly around the round room's periphery. Entitled "The

[2] An exhibition of real human specimens preserved through Plastination.

Maim and the Miracle," the exhibit had initially opened to commemorate the Battle of Shiloh's 150th anniversary. It educates the public on the horrors of Civil War battlefield medicine. Cases clustered near the room's center hold assorted authentic artifacts like a lead slug some nameless Yankee had been told to bite down upon while a doctor with a flimsy saw proceeded to amputate his leg. From the press boards leer enlarged graphics of grisly amputation techniques, including the circular amputation, wherein a small knife is used to cut in a circular fashion all around and through the skin and muscle surrounding a bone, before a hacksaw finishes the job. A hooked tenaculum then pulls the arteries from the stump, that they might be tied off and the spiral tourniquet unbound, the flap sewn closed, and the patient sent to (hopefully) mend sans antibiotics.

Yes, this has been Lorrie's porn for five years running. Five years as CCO. Five years of lunch breaks spent wandering around the museum's antechambers, watching people who didn't know they were being watched, noting their habits, admiring well-behaved kiddos who quietly, studiously read each exhibit placard, and quietly, studiously cursing those who used flash photography to snap selfies with the freestanding wax figures, the "No Flash Photography Allowed" sign clearly photobombing the background of each pic. Meandering backstage of the theater, nodding Hi to the actors in their period dress, then always arriving, irresistibly drawn back to, the Red Room; memorizing each diagram and rusty dull blade, every cracked glass vial still half-full of opium—medicines that almost two hundred years after their production cause heinous chemical burns when you accidentally drop a vial during install. Vials from a kit marked Dr. Braker, Remarkable Remedies, 1863.

Morphine, a substance in opium, is still used in hospitals today. People still get addicted to it, all of us looking to kill the pain; or in Lorrie's case, to induce it.

Quickly, she finishes in the stall, flushes the toilet, washes her hands. Heads back to her office, back to work, where she usually feels satisfied for a full hour before her thoughts worm roguishly back to her right hand, click-clacking expertly against the keys, producing short press-friendly paragraph after productive paragraph, and yet—so useless.

That arm, those tapering fingers; an ordinary limb, even attractive, but unnecessary!

What keeps Lorrie from performing an auto-amputation? The gesture, which one could make a limited number of times, would be meaningless and not half so enjoyable, she feels sure, if executed alone, without a partner, without an audience.

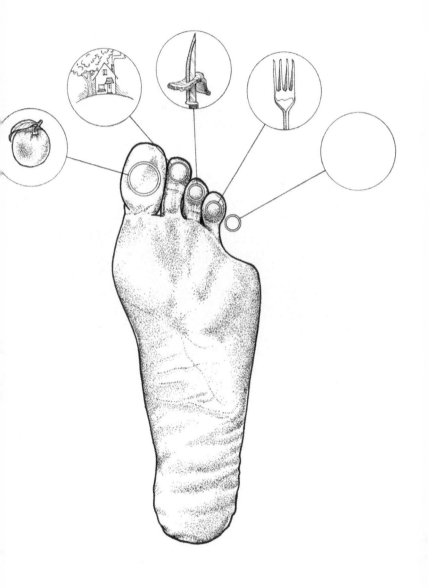

On Tuesday, Lorrie drives to Chicago, her hours on the state's dime, her mileage to be reimbursed. When she isn't writing press releases she fills in as artifact courier, personally overseeing the packaging and shuttling of artifacts on loan from the home institution to her presidential museum. Normally the couriering is a contract lackey's job, but state budget cuts mean more and more that the work load is high and the available hands scarce (another reason to keep her own!) and so full-time staff go in lieu as needed.

Lorrie's assignment is to pick up an 1888 Harrison-Cleveland silk campaign flag from the Field Museum's[3] textile collection and see it safely back to Springfield by 5:00 PM. Given that the round trip takes 7 hours on a good day, she has just over an hour to meet with the Field's Collections Manager, and scrounge food to eat in the car on the way back. What a day.

Lorrie sips her black coffee and checks her black eyeliner in the rearview mirror and sings Stevie Nicks songs all the way to the Windy City, just because she can.

---

[3] The Field Museum of Natural History, Chicago.

On Tuesday, **TRICE** is in the Pentagon's janitorial closet, the only room without video surveillance in the whole compound. He's fucking a nurse against a shelving unit of bottles and toilet paper. Only she's a zombie nurse. Only it's Halloween and the face paint and ridiculous getup help disguise that she's the First Lady, the wife of the fucking president of the United States. A wobbly bottle of Windex finally falls over with a thud. Trice stops thrusting long enough to make sure no one who matters has overhead. "Hey, keep it down!" the janitor-lookout loud-whispers from the hallway.

Trice had fixed the janitor's son up with a robotics apparatus that ultimately won for the boy the state science fair and a scholarship to a good school. Even the Pentagon's janitors barely make a living wage, but now his son is going places. In the hallway they hear the janitor chuckle. In the hallway the janitor doesn't hear another sound. Government officials are nothing if not discreet about their indiscretions—it's usually not their fault when they're finally exposed.

As a bio-mechanical engineer, Trice understands at a glance how things—especially bodies—work. All the interlocking parts, the balls and sockets, the tarsals and metatarsals, the pistoning muscles and the small, vibrating bones of the inner ear canal, one called a stirrup. He tells the First Lady as she pulls her nurse's skirt back down that he'd like to put her in stirrups and take a vibrating something to a small other something until it isn't so small anymore. She laughs softly and rolls her eyes. "Use your words, Trice." Then she's gone. He doesn't know when he'll see her next, but she always gives him the signal. They never meet in the same place twice.

On Tuesday, **CAPTAIN HOOK** nearly blows off his other arm. To a glass beaker full of potassium chlorate he adds two drops too many of sulfuric acid. Bartholomew never excelled at science in school, but as an adult he's learned a new appreciation for chemistry in particular, fascinated for the first time by the fact that heavy metals can also be gases, that gases can be pressurized (he knew this principle well enough from war—a gun merely channels a gas-pressured force in one direction), and that pressure can be so precisely calibrated as to explode magnificently at exactly the desired moment.

In the mountain there is a cave.

In the cave there is a man.

In the man there is an unbroken concentration upon the cave wall, which he gazes at all day and all night while "seeing" nothing whatsoever.

The man's name is **YUPTAG**, and he meditates on and for eternal life.

One day, **A GIRL** approaches the cave entrance. She sees Yuptag and is not afraid. She asks him what he is doing. He makes no reply. She sits beside him and for a whole day stares at the self-same wall. She leaves when the sun goes down.

The next day, the girl returns with the dawn and a knife.

"Teach me," she demands.

When Yuptag still makes no reply, she brings the knife down *thwifft* through her other outstretched arm, severing it completely. Throwing the arm at the man, the girl leaves the cave.

The next day, the girl again returns with the dawn and a knife. Yuptag still sits where he always sits, staring the same intent stare. Standing directly in front of the man, the girl brings the knife to her throat with her one good hand.

"Teach me," she demands.

For the first time, Yuptag's eyes focus on the girl.

"Okay," he agrees. "We begin by sitting."

The girl sits next to the man and she learns.

Every Sunday night, **DON** leads a veterans' support group next door to the presidential museum. A farmer and lay chaplain trained in tenets of most major world religions, he's never seen war except through the memories of a dozen haunted men of all ages, having served a combined 29 tours in 14 different countries. Some of them are amputees. One is paralyzed from the neck down. All still feel like they are sometimes back in the line of fire, sending and dodging bullets. Watching out for their soldier-brothers. Watching out for themselves.

Because when they were deployed they never could relax, not for a minute, not fully—alert even when they were sleeping to the echoing sounds of engines and waiting, always and unconsciously waiting, for the next bomb to explode somewhere far off or right overhead, right under your buddy's foot as he took one ill-conceived step too many. Because they can not otherwise relax they drink coffee at these meetings, and stay as wide-eyed and jumpy as they ever were, chemically fighting a tiredness that, if entertained, would swallow them whole.

"Ralph," Don prompts quietly. "You're up."

RALPH has been concentrating all night on the wall. The wall is cinderblock, painted gray, clean but unremarkable in this bookstore basement. There is nothing at which to stare.

"Ralph," Don's soft voice comes again, when it seems the 45-year-old Gulf War[4] vet is not going to respond. "Want to tell us what you're seeing?"

This tactic is a favorite of the just-graying chaplain's to lift the pressure off personal share time. If the guys (and women when applicable, though there are none present tonight) could let their thoughts play like a movie, and if

---

[4] Codenamed "Operation Desert Shield (2 August 1990-17 January 1991) and "Operation Desert Storm" (17 January 1991-28 February 1991).

they could learn to reframe those thoughts as something removed and cinematic, it anesthetized somehow the bite of the personal. They could describe the scene as they would that of any film, and then it was only sharing art, only talking about the writing and the actors' expressions and the director's stylistic choices and the producer's vision.

Like some movies do, it might feel real, but like all movies do, it would eventually end—and that's what Don taught them to do: watch their mind-movies; there was something to be learned. Then turn them off and go to bed and rest, goddammit, rest; they deserved it.

Finally Ralph speaks. "It's 1991. I know because we're all wearing Desert Night Camouflage, but we've seen pictures of the new uniforms with the Three Color Desert print and we got those the very next month.

"There's a woman in the room, very pretty. Blonde hair in a bun, straight back. She's my superior, and anyway there's no fraternizing, so I don't talk to her, only stand at attention and pretend I don't overhear what she's telling the Lieutenant Colonel. Kaylee is her name. 1st Lieutenant **KAYLEE BRIGHT**. She's briefing the LC on a new technology, some kind of bioluminescent application. You fly low over the ground, spraying a sticky mist. At night it glows. The idea is that anywhere someone's disturbed the soil, say to plant an IED, we could see it, right? They'd have broken the surface of the application. It'd show like a dark spot. It sounded pretty good.

"The LC ordered Kaylee to go on a test run that night, to accompany the pilot who earlier that day had sprayed the stuff. They'd fly back over, and see what they could see."

Ralph pauses. Breathes. Continues.

"In the next scene, Kaylee's in the copilot's chair when a rocket launcher blows the wing clean off their tiny plane. The craft dips then nosedives, straight into the sand they were skimming but 50 yards above. The sheet metal crumples like an accordion, like a Chinese finger trap inhaling, expanding, finally ballooning into flame.

"Kaylee doesn't feel the fire because the plane's window frame cut her head clean off upon impact. Not even her bun came undone."

Fiddling with her bun in the bathroom mirror, **LORRIE** wonders why she always looks so pallid on camera. Any more make-up and the clown effect would be worse, so she supposes there is nothing for it. Except perhaps a beach vacation. Five long days of UV and Tanqueray. Maybe she'll see if they need a courier for any loans from the University of Florida's art department. Just head down there and—

"You ready?" a male voice calls from outside the door.

It is the cameraman, and Lorrie thinks again that it's the museum director's job to make media appearances, not her own. She's only supposed to write the damn scripts.

Lorrie exits, and teeters on uncustomary heels across the museum atrium. She stands where they tell her to stand, across from the wax figure First Family and next to a new display case holding a just-acquired document from an auction in New South Wales. It never fails to surprise her how many bits of material history find their way across whole oceans, into the hands of collectors with fetishistic interests; or who just know a good thing when they see one. This document is a handwritten letter from Dr. Horace C. Braker—the same Braker whose rotting leather medical kits full of powdery white vials are permanently displayed in the Civil War medicine exhibit. In the Red Room.

Lorrie begins: "What you see here is a letter from Dr. Braker to his wife, who was at their home in Rhode Island. The letter reads like most others in the Braker paper collection: long lists, heavy on procedure and instrument inventory. Dr. Braker had planned to write a book on battlefield medicine once the war was over. As you can see (and here the camera zooms in for a close-up), this particular letter catalogues the surgical implements included in a new kit Braker had just received from Boston."

The anchor prompts her: "Can you read some of those descriptions for us? I understand they're quite graphic."

"Sure," Lorrie replies, "though they're not graphic so much as medically accurate."

They're only words, and words stripped of their context are only sounds. But something about those sounds resonates primally with the core of Lorrie's being.

"Six-inch serrated," Lorrie reads, and all those sensual esses pool like drool in her mouth. She swallows quickly, the way you do after having other 6-inch things in your mouth, so as not to choke, or gag—unless that's the point—but not on TV for Christ's sake. Lorrie feels glad that her sleeveless blouse is high-necked, with a pretty, ruffled front. They won't see her reddening chest, and it might distract from her pinkening face, and anyway, who hears the word "sharp" and thinks "sex?" Only freaks.

She shakes her head. The anchorman is asking her another question.

In the palace there is an aging warrior.

In the warrior there is a secret.

The wisdom-bomb he is about to drop will be deadly. But it could save many more lives.

"When you think of war," **YUPTAG** admonishes, "you think of glory. You think in archaic terms of an 'us' and a 'them,' of vanquishing an enemy. If you acknowledge the bloodshed at all, it is whatever percentage you deem an 'acceptable necessity.' It's not real to you, here, now, until you're in the middle of it, there, then."

The warrior parts his robe, revealing a ghastly, self-inflicted stomach wound. With a moan, he reaches into the cut, grabbing ropes of offal, drawing them out.

"This is your reality check. Visceral destruction." He chokes on the blood now flowing from his mouth. "Literal decay."

Yuptag looks around at his comrades lining the room. "Do not let my death be in vain."

In 2003, Melody Gilbert[5] made a documentary called *Whole*. It's a UK film and hard to find in America. Even harder to find on the internet. Is it that well-policed or does nobody care except for the film's stars? Men with missing legs due to intentional gunshot wounds, as only in dismemberment could they feel, at last, whole.

Doctors call it Body Integrity Identity Disorder (BIID).[6] Maybe there's a place where the wires crossed, where the signals aren't transmitting correctly, and so limbs feel "extra," not of the self.

That guy, does he see couples holding hands and wish he had a hand? Does he see the girl put her legs, two, in her boyfriend's lap, and think if nature gave us two, and everyone else is doing it—walking, eating, loving—with two—

---

[5] Documentary filmmaker and professor of film at the American University in Bulgaria.

[6] A psychological disorder in which an otherwise healthy individual feels that s/he is meant to be disabled.

Facts about American Amputees:

You have upper extremity and lower extremity amputees and the occasional bouncing torso we call a nugget. You have transradial and transhumeral depending: above or below the elbow; depending on whether a shoulder disarticulation means the ribs end their starfish seige at the back or there's more.beyond.continuing. You have partial hands with so much or so little as a piece of one digit missing (Ada McGrath's silver-soldered fingers in Jane Campion's[7] *The Piano*, for example—silly woman trying to kill herself despite having a daughter, having George the tattooed Maori man with a man butt that actually looks good naked [rare]). You furthermore have transtibial or transfemoral depending on: above or below the knee.

Among Americans, 80% of lower extremity amputations are due to poor vascular conditioning (diabetes). A small fraction, trauma (war vets; farming or lawnmower accidents).

Among Americans, the majority of upper extremity amputations are due to trauma (war vets; farming or lawnmower accidents). 300 Americans are double-arm amputees. They were electrical lines-people or other victims of their trade.

Some number of Americans contract some disease annually. The bacteria makes the body reject its own extremities. Slow suffocation of, rotting away of, extraneous parts falling lopsided at inopportune moments.

Sunflower seastars[8] contracting Sea Star Wasting Syndrome twist their arms into knots, send the arms

---

[7] A New Zealand screenwriter, producer, and director.

[8] Among the largest sea stars in the world, Sunflower seastars have 16 to 24 limbs with a maximum armspan of 3.3 ft.

HEADCHEESE

crawling away, until the arms tear off of the body, spilling offal. They rip themselves apart. They die within 24
hours. Citizens spotting the bodies are encouraged to
tweet #SickStarfish.

Color in the rectified socket, the liner sleeve, the
locked and articulating joints. Shade the socket the color
of connection between the residual limb and device, the
lining the white of rubber, the black of a silicone sleeve,
fitting tight, fitting sweaty, you want to take it off for sex.

I smell how synthetic material intensifies the human
smell of you. It grows the bacteria that eats limbs.

If you don't have one? (A limb.)

Who asked about penises? Penises are not [are] a limb.

Chuck P.[9] wrote a story about biting and choking and
the ghosts that haunt people when they lock each other
in a room but convince themselves that someone else has
the key.

Color the custom-molded fit of the rectified socket
a color that reveals more about your psyche than you
realize. Pull the fiberglass fitting on like a rigid pair
of underwear, a second skin, a second limb. Become a
walker, a **SKINWALKER**, and know that no matter how
tight the fiberglass rods, the 3D-printed bolts and pegs,
the electro-myographic nodes at raw skin points of attachment, *twitch twitch fast-twitch*, the device will weigh
as much as a flesh-and-bone foot (4-5 pounds) with an
ankle and lower calf (10 pounds) from the knee down
(20 pounds), also a shoe. It's all for balance, or a weighted
sense of self. Wait for a sense of self to return, to engage
for Madonna's[10] very first time, reruns on Gagavision[11]

[9] An American novelist and freelance journalist.

[10] An American singer, songwriter, actress, and businesswoman.

[11] On the Haus of Gaga app, webisodes in which American singer-song-
writer Lady Gaga discusses her fashion inspirations and the works
created by the Haus design team.

and the shellaceous points of a cone bra, leopard leotard, silver hot pants, stripper heels (they're more comfortable; you can wear them for longer).

The leg has its weight-bearing load, plus the stressures of acceleration, walking, maybe a curved carbon fiber rod for the amputee runner. If you didn't want the leg, you probably don't want to run, and what if you had a debilitating fear of pain? Would the pain outweigh the desire for orgasm? Isn't all pain sexual? Do surgeons study medicine because they're sadomasochists, committed to the moment over eight long years of the first scalpel-slice open, the first needle-and-thread piercing of, sewing of, a severed limb.finger.toe back onto the body? That whole head transplant, will it actually work? Will the eyelids flutter and how many capillaries will that mean re-attaching, how many spinal nerves?

No more and no less than the first cut.

First human head amputation and transplant, scheduled for 2017, in China, by an Italian doctor,[12] on a Russian man[13] with muscular dystrophy who wants a new body.

Who wants a new body?

A "better" body, like **LORRIE**—she only wanted a better body when she stepped on the music box. I wonder, for all the body-shaming and eating disorders we manifest, if everyone switched out their bodies for ones they liked better, would they see them through the same infected, disillusioned eyes and be as dissatisfied?

Is it all in the damn head?

---

[12] Sergio Canavero.

[13] Valery Spiridonov.

GEORGE MA'IITSOH is 76 years old when he develops tinnitus,[14] a persistent and just-loud-enough-to-drive-you-absolutely-crazy ringing of the ears, particularly his left ear, which sometimes refuses to let him sleep at night. Because he has always suffered in silence (strong by nature, silent by choice) he does not tell his daughter or his grandkids, does not ask them to take him to see a specialist (aging by nature, no longer able to drive himself not by choice). Because George is Navajo, he knows it is not nerve damage but another world, a half-animal world trying to contact this one. The ringing occasionally morphs into static and in its deeper noise he can almost hear words, isolated out-of-context phrases, and maybe what sounds like a name. It makes George hate his ears, little brown appendages, better anymore at drowning out the world than letting in sweet birdsong or the echoes that live only in memory of **SARAH**'s humming. When he tries to recall it, tries to hear her in his head, the static-y ringing only seems to grow louder. Once, in a hospital waiting room, George caught an episode of *True Emergencies* on TV, about a man who'd compulsively driven screwdrivers into his brain through his ear. Miraculously, he lived—and George thinks about it: about getting rid of his ears, his used-to-be-perfectly-ordinary nature-given ears that now feel cursed by Niltsi[15] himself.

George had been in the waiting room that day because his daughter had been giving birth to George's first grandson. He had never been in a hospital before. It was maybe the tenth time ever he'd watched TV.

George lives on a reservation in Arizona and avoids the wider world as much as he can. Sometimes he reads

---

[14] The hearing of sound when no external sound is present.

[15] Navajo wind god.

a book, but mostly he walks, more slowly these days, around Mt. Icaro's rocky base, tracking wildlife for fun and collecting herbs for function. George feels sure he'll make a poultice yet that will stop, stop, stop the tinnitus.

It used to be that George taught in the Native American Institute's storytelling program, "borrowing the 'oral' from 'sex,'" he liked to quip, "and putting it back into history." Despite George's aversion to modern American culture, he is neither ignorant nor a prude; the way he and Sarah used to make love could have started a prairie fire for its heat and intensity. He just knows that young adults only hear what old folks like himself say if he speaks in their language—their vulgar, Christianized (weaponized), whitebread language. He supposes someday even Navajo will die out. When you don't use something, you lose it. Now only the gangs spit some hybridized form of Navajo like code talk because no one else can understand it.

Outside, the sun sets on another day. George has walked nine miles looking for snakeweed;[16] he's tired and ready for rest. On cue, the tinnitus sounds a quiet little cowbell, just janky enough to let George know: this will be a very long night after all. He claps palms with red dirt yet in their grooves against traitorous ears, thinking only, "You will not, you must not, win."

---

[16] *Gutierrezia sarothrae.*

I had my
"body correction" on April 27
"punished" by shock therapy under
forcible detainment.
with "it"—don't know what to call
intentional episodic injury by
electric drill.
more relaxed and able to socialize, I
saw my amputee neighbor, a dad
loved by his kids.

totally absorbed by need,
loved ones feel betrayed—married
under "false pretenses"
marriage, kids, career: instants of joy but
never enough

dry ice relieved fifty years of torment
what "should" and "should not" be there
guillotines
mutilation vs.
the 21st century

my "little leg"
is a nose job
is a radiator clamp and
circular saw.

On Wednesday, **GEORGE** shows back up at his old stomping grounds, the Institute. Invited to guest-lecture on the Navajo Way, George had at first graciously declined. *The Navajo Way?* he thought. Asking Navajo kids to attend a lecture on themselves was like telling a Muslim girl to attend a class on the Pakistani Way. Ridiculous, wasn't it? So the metaphor wasn't perfect. Many Muslim girls couldn't even attend school, and if they could there was the public school-private school disparity, and all kinds of wealth inequity, and the Muslim-Hindu hostility, and yes, there were always things to learn by having your culture reflected back to you. Certainly more than the loss of a tribal language had changed between 1945 and the tight blue jeans-wearing youth of 2015. George knew immediately where to start his lecture, which would be strictly oral, no electronic slides, aided if need be by stick figures drawn in the fucking sand. He'd start with those elements of the Navajo Way perfectly immune to time and its changes: the **SKINWALKER** mythos.

George introduces skinwalkers to a class of 12 initially bored (perpetually jaded) students with—what else?—a story.

"The night I was conceived," George begins, "there was no moon. But the stars shone so brightly that it may have been daylight reflected through a billion teenage pores." Some of the kids chuckle shortly, unsure if laughter is the correct response.

Dogson[17] says you only have to think of something intently enough to manifest it. All this researching amputation has manifested—well, not amputations (that I know of), but friends sending me videos and article links, Reddit threads and black-and-white photos of a headless chicken named Mike.[18]

Seems when Lloyd Olsen[19] cut Mike's head off, he aimed a little high, leaving one ear and the chicken's brainstem intact. The brainstem supports the autonomic functions, so even if Mike no longer was conscious of being alive, live he did, attempting to peck and crow like other fry roosters. Olsen fed him with an eyedropper through the gaping hole of Mike's exposed throat, used another eyedropper to suck the mucus away (it gurgled whenever Mike tried to crow) and when Mike continued living, Olsen took him on tour, sure his sideshow sidekick would be the key to his retirement.

If it goes that way for the Russian in China (though it won't—the procedure requires severing the brainstem), we wouldn't be allowed to parade him like a freak attraction, the man who eats, moans, and gets erections—all without a head! On literal autopilot until the body died, of neglect or old age or someone forgetting to suck with a silicone bulb the snot from Spiridonov's neck hole. The kind of science experiment that we no longer allow in this country. In China, still most everything goes.

---

[17] American anti-novelist.

[18] Also known as Miracle Mike, a Wyandotte chicken that lived for 18 months after his head had been cut off.

[19] Farmer from Fruita, Colorado.

All of **CAPTAIN HOOK**'s science experiments are legal within the confines of his lab, illegal outside its walls, and downright treasonous beyond the compound's perimeter. He starts small—liquid nitrogen bombs "to go." Using a stainless steel sphere no bigger than a fizzing bath bomb and resembling somewhat a Pokéball,[20] its dual chambers kept isolated until the appointed time by a thin sheet of aluminized mylar easily perforated, the bomb would be the over-the-counter version of Percocet: easy to replicate and distribute, and precise in its target benefit. When a button in the sphere's exterior is depressed (and real pressure must be applied, not just your accidental bump), an internal punch creates a hole between the chambers, allowing dry ice to mix with 99% isopropyl alcohol. The result? Poor man's liquid nitrogen. Put the bomb in a plastic bag with your leg, a single finger, whatever you wish to "lose"—the greater the limb loss, the more significant the endorphin rush. An adult leg will freeze solid within two hours, the flesh too badly damaged at that point to save. Tell the doctor to cut it off and sew you up, and if he tries to save it anyway, threaten to hobble out, let it rot, and drop off. Gangrene is serious business.

---

[20] A spherical device used by Pokémon Trainers to capture wild Pokémon and store them in the player's inventory when not active.

There are three amputees in the veterans' support group, including **DON**. One voluntary, two involuntary. A vet wounded in a war and forever after handicapped, taunted by phantom limb pains, plagued by arthritis and nightmares, looks at the man who shot his own leg off with the sense of a waking nightmare. No way he can be lucid (who would DO that?). He tries to tell himself it was an accident or a coward's move: probably Zed only meant to shoot through his foot, be discharged and taken to the VA clinic, missing weeks in the trench so to collect the remaining pieces of his sanity. It would be a coward's move, but one Ralph could at least fathom.

"Was that it, Zed?" Ralph asks. "You only meant to shoot your foot?"

"Hell naw," Zed says with a grin. "Shotgun, right through the top of my knee. Lost everything below and a good bit above the joint." Leaning forward, Zed whispers conspiratorially: "It's called transfemoral. Where they made the cut, I mean."

Ralph's stomach rolls. "Zed, I don't think it's such a good idea for you to come to group anymore."

"What? Why?"

"The guys … they all think you're a war vet."

"I am!"

"Yeah, but they think that's how you lost your leg. How can you support amputee victims, when yours was …" Ralph swallows hard. "Self-inflicted?"

"Maybe I'm the best person for it. I'm happy every goddamn day that I only have one leg. I'm more 'me,' more peaceful than I've ever been. I can help other vets find that peace, too. I can help them feel whole."

Ralph stirs a thin white line of cream into his coffee. He takes all new members out for coffee to make them feel welcome. The more comfortable they feel in group, the more they open up about their history. The more they open up, the more healing can actually occur. "So tell me your story, man."

peg legs :: pigeons on the roof :: fried eggs on a hot plate ::
salt and pepper packets neatly arranged in the drawer :: smells
like whiskey and wood shavings :: cabinet maker :: hand-tooled
peg with tanned hide straps and brass buckles :: Halloween ::
Renaissance fair :: shavings for a pet rat

"Kommen."

ZED the German cabinet-maker lays one callused
dirty hand palm-up on the table. His fingernails are long
and brown-brittle as Manky's, his pet rat. It is with the
soft click of nail on nail that Manky steps into Zed's palm.
Scooping him up, Zed sets the rat on his shoulder like a
pirate does his parrot. He feeds Manky a bit of scrambled
egg. Pats his head. Clomps across the kitchen's broken
brown-tiled floor on his wooden peg leg, also like a pirate and his parrot.

Everything in this scene is brown. Zed's long, ratty
(pun-intended) hair. The strip of rawhide that ties said
hair back messily. Zed's teeth are brown. The counter on
which he knocks another capful of brown whiskey into
his darker brown coffee (sloshing in a chipped brown
Corningware mug) is speckled brown formica. The waf-
fles are burned brown and brown grime is smeared across
the windows, caked in the corners. Caked as the cake of
thick brown soap that has never made anything cleaner—only streakier. Brown is the plastic wall-mounted
phone that doesn't ring, its service disconnected long ago.
Brown are the wooden cabinets that alone gleam with a
curious inner radiance. This wood was loved. Pulled one
plank at a time into planar perfection. Straight, smart, and
pretty to look at. The opposite altogether of Zed's crudely
hand-hewn peg leg carved for utility and nicked with the
futility of trying to keep any well-worn thing sacred.

"My parents, E. and M., were young then."

GEORGE does not mention that just last night he dreamed of a massive cougar. In the vision, he was playing Ring-the-Stick with his brother at night, when the moon picked out a pair of glinting eyes and then the powerfully hunched shoulders of a feral cat in silent ambush. The boys backed slowly, so slowly away—but as George knew, if a cougar let itself be seen, it was already too late for you. George choked on his cry as with one swift leap the cougar fastened its unapologetic jaws around B.'s neck, ripping a wide, red hole in his brother's throat. Fighting with everything he had against the dream paralysis that held him, George finally awoke with a pained yell. "Help!" seemed to hang in the 2 AM air, its echo growing louder the longer George listened. It'd been hours before he fell asleep again. By that time, dawn was breaking blood red in the east.

"Though later their relationship soured, I can only imagine they were very close that evening, wrapped in bed, my father reading, as was his habit, a book aloud to my mother before they slept.

"That's when M. heard it the first time: a thump, then the distinct sound of footsteps across the roof. Freezing, she gripped my father's arm beside her. 'E., did you hear that?'"

E. paused in his reading but quickly resumed, having heard nothing. Had he looked at his wife's face, he would've known something was wrong. He did when it happened again.

Many, many movies through the years have treated the theme of amputation. In horror movies, it's usually disguised as mutilation. The original *Texas Chain Saw Massacre*[21] went there in the early '70s. Subsequent remakes have upped the gore factor and cut most semblance of a storyline. The 1974 version opens with a crazy slaughterhouse employee. He describes the process for making headcheese.

Simmer the head for three hours with:
1 heaping teaspoon of peppercorn
4 stalks of celery
large bunch of garden herbs (e.g. parsley & thyme)
2 bay leaves
4 large garlic cloves
2 star anise
1 teaspoon whole allspice

Remove head skin.

Remove head meat.

Build the head cheese. Place head meat in loaf pan, layered with herbs and enough stock to rise and congeal in fridge.

Set for four hours.

Unmold. Slice with a very sharp knife.

Serve with fresh bread, crackers, and cheese.

---

[21] A 1974 American horror film, The Texas Chainsaw Massacre follows a group of friends who fall victim to a family of cannibals while on their way to visit an old homestead. Although it was marketed as a true story to attract a wider audience and as a subtle commentary on the era's political climate, its plot is entirely fictional; however, the character of Leatherface and minor plot details were inspired by the crimes of real-life murderer Ed Gein.

They don't make poultry head cheese, only bovine and pork. Maybe because of the relative size? Mike's head traveled with him in a glass jar of preservative, a spectacle and a wonder but never a delicacy.

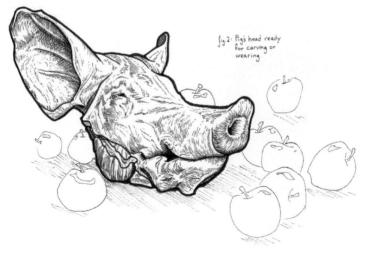

fig. 2: Pig's head ready for carving or wearing

In the Philippines, chicken beak (balut) is a delicacy.

Take one fertilized chicken or duck egg.

Boil for 15 minutes.

Remove shell.

Dine on compressed beak, veins, developing wings.

The 2006 film *Texas Chainsaw Massacre: The Beginning*[22] features Leatherface cutting off his uncle's legs at the knee. The father was already immobile, following around in his wheelchair. His legs perfectly positioned for the slice-through of a barbed chain turning at 60 miles per hour. The blood spurted theatrically and without tourniquets the man should have died.

But it was a movie.

True-to-life circular saw amputee Sandra[23] appeared on Jerry Springer in 2007. A male-to-female transexual and BIID sufferer (though that term didn't yet exist), Sandra tried lesser methods for a time, like hammering nails into her lower leg bones, hoping to spur an infection before finally tightening hose clamps around her thighs and firing up the power tool. Jerry Springer ran a circular saw while walking up the aisle through the audience, just so everyone could hear that sound and cringe at Sandra's story.

Sandra has no regrets.

---

[22] A remake of *The Texas Chain Saw Massacre* and the sixth entry in *The Texas Chainsaw Massacre* franchise.

[23] Season 16, episode 29, "I'm Happy I Cut Off My Legs!" Aired 2 November 2006.

LORRIE's pet frog Larry burps a hello when she enters the room and goodnight when she turns out the light. The little UV bulb in his tank stays on, and filtering through the aerated water, light bubbles play over Lorrie's ceiling in the darkness. The frog had not been her idea. Lorrie inherited Larry from her best friend's kid, just before they moved to Delaware and couldn't take him. Why don't you just let him go free? Lorrie had asked seven-year-old M. M. had launched into a lengthy treatise on domesticated vs. feral animals and so fearing for little Larry's inevitable death by hawk should she turn him out, Lorrie had been guilted into accepting the thing despite the fact that every time she looked at Larry she thought about dissection.

In eighth grade science they'd all run scalpels through the bellies of dead frogs, wearing latex gloves and masks against the poison residues of formaldehyde, and with tiny metal rods had prodded, some gingerly and some roguishly, through the inner machinations of respiratory, digestive, and reproductive systems not too dissimilar from their own. They stuck pushpins through the specimens' outer limbs, crucifying each frog on a rubber mat, instructed to snap the delicate bones if they weren't cooperating.

That night, Lorrie's mum had served frog legs for dinner, and the abhorrence Lorrie had contained all day at school had rushed out of her in a thick stream of bile, drowning the legs, making them float and kick upon her plate.

Just keep swimming.

As a high schooler, Lorrie would take her boyfriends to the pond on her grandparents' farm, where they'd sweaty-fuck in the long grass, assaulted by mosquitoes, and after, she'd hold their lighters against the water's surface, and watch for the dark outlines of tadpoles swimming. She couldn't understand what happened to their tails—they didn't shed them, but absorbed them as they transformed into frogs. She wondered if ever the legs just failed to grow, a genetic flaw. If frogs needed their legs—and what the evolutionary adaptation had looked like there. She thought about concentrating really, really hard until her own leg—*thwup*—absorbed back into her body like a remnant fetal tail. She thought about how some babies were born having not reabsorbed their tails, how the doctors cut them off. She wondered what they did with the tails. She thought about Rose Siggins,[24] the woman born without any legs at all, just a torso who knuckled around on over-developed arms. Rose was, as Lady Gaga affirmed, "born that way / God makes no mistakes." But Lorrie felt like a mistake, a big one. A malformed abomination. To hear that Rose would wish for legs if she could have them, but there were no stumps, no sockets to which to attach/insert prostheses. Lorrie would sigh and shake her head and her boyfriend of the month would ask what was wrong, if he was sensitive, or say, "Hey, baby, wanna go again?" if he was not. The crude ones would tell her she was hot and the thoughtful ones would tell her she was beautiful and as they fit themselves together she wondered why nothing fit at all.

---

[24] An American actress born with sacral agenesis.

Neil Strauss[25] wrote a book called *The Game: Penetrating the Secret Society of Pick-Up Artists* that—and this is a sex-positive feminist speaking here—taught men how to get all the tail (there's that vestigial part again—why?) they wanted without any kind of commitment. *The Game* espouses making fun of women and other kinds of reverse (perverse) psychology—and for non-religious men everywhere, it became their Bible. Last year, Strauss came out with another book that chronicled his legit sex addiction and apologized in a sorry-not sorry way for his warped view of women, which he attributed to his relationship with his mother.

Neil's mother is an amputee, and his father had an amputee fetish. Mr. Strauss was forever trying to exploit his wife's image in certain circles. Mrs. Strauss of course grew bitter and resentful, and soon substituted her son's attentions for her emotionally unavailable husband's. Though the mother-son relationship never became physical, it was emotionally intimate in a way reserved for most adults and shielded from most children. Neil hated his father and probably had an Oedipal complex for his mother ... and his was the psychology that resonated with millions of men and made *The Game* an international bestseller, undoing a century's work toward gender equality in a couple months' time.

---

[25] An American author, journalist, and ghostwriter best known for his book *The Game: Penetrating the Secret Society of Pickup Artists*, in which he describes his experiences in the seduction community in an effort to become a "pick-up artist."

Porn comes in all types and styles. There's heterosexual, homosexual, pansexual, and zoophile porn. Solo masturbation, couples, strangers, threesomes, and groups. Anime, tentacle, robot, and Sybian. Wide-angle, hidden camera, and point-of view. Coeds and hazing, kiddies and abuse, grandpas and MILFs and interracial grannies. Anal and dildo and DP and beads, pissing and squirting and shitting and milk enemas. There are porn clips that actually are or only claim to be snuff films. There are films where limbs get amputated on-screen, either with or without the star's permission, and occasionally midway through, the blood spatter needs to be wiped from the lens.

Two Girls, One Cup[26] and the closely-related horror film *The Human Centipede*[27] are about coprophilia—the love of shit. Some wannabe-amputees inject their limbs with syringes full of their own feces. Like the hammer and nail method, the idea is to infect the flesh and bone beyond the point of saving, rendering amputation advisable and (hopefully, the wannabe thinks, crossing the fingers of his non-festering hand) absolutely necessary. Bacteria are tricky little bastards though. Your blood vessels are the perfect vehicle for any infection to go systemic. A body-wide waterslide for E. Coli to party down.

[26] A 2007 Brazilian scat-fetish pornographic film.

[27] A 2009 Dutch horror film, it tells the story of a German doctor who kidnaps three tourists and joins them surgically, mouth to anus, forming a "human centipede."

On Tuesday, TRICE hangs out with the Resurrected, a group of gamers with whom he'd prefer to never be publicly associated (though it's not like a sex scandal or anything). He tells them his name is Julian, and that he works at a coffee shop on U Street. When they start mega-sessions of D&D, his character is usually a dwarf with only one arm, who has replaced his missing limb with a self-sharpening battle axe.

One Tuesday, after the guys finish up a grueling four-week long session of the game, someone suggests they play Guillotine.[28]

Guillotine is a card game set during—when else—the French Revolution, where you try to collect the heads of as many nobles as possible and spare the townsfolk. It's very antidisestablishmentarian that way. Marie Antoinette is worth the most points of course, and you also do well by collecting cards of a certain color. The storyline spans multiple 'days' but it may take only 15 minutes to play a complete game.

Antoine Louis[29] invented the guillotine contraption and Wizards of the Coast invented the Guillotine game. Joseph-Ignace Guillotin,[30] the man for whom the contraption was named, later lost his head to the device. Always a scientist, Guillotin turned even his death into an experiment—the last contribution he would ever make to society. "After the blade drops," he said, then blinking eyelids, speaking, moving eyes, movement of the mouth.

He did not invent the guillotine nor did he support the death penalty—but for suggesting the guillotine as a more humane form of capital punishment than the wheel,

---

[28] A card game created by Wizards of the Coast, released on Bastille Day 1998.

[29] 1723-1792.

[30] 1738-1814.

or burning at the stake, he got his.

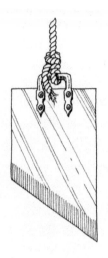

On Wednesday, **LORRIE** dons her very best clubwear: a skintight black lace mini with a dangerous slit up the back, rivets around the neckline, and thumbholes in the sheer lace sleeves. She steps into black suede high-heeled booties, slicks her hair back, applies dark lipstick and a ridiculous gold Yoda necklace. The effect is half-sex kitten, half-kitsch vixen, and she feels hella good. It's a nice night, so she walks the five blocks to the downtown square, bookended by the museum to the east, condos to the west, and a row of bars at the southern border, spreading further south into city lights and the promise that warm nights always hold.

She passes homeless panhandlers and college students already drunk, nods to each, and listens to the clink of copper bangles at her right wrist only sway in step with her boots—pretending for the night that her left arm isn't there. The orange buzz of the streetlamps gives way to an identical orange backlighting of the bar's mirror in Lorrie's favorite midtown speakeasy. If Tim Burton and the Quay Brothers ever made a film together, it would look like the art on these walls: an accumulated collage of New Age paintings, vintage signs and circus posters, orphaned mannequin parts, cue balls, jacks, spiders, stamped pewter lanterns in every jewel-toned tint of Moroccan glass, charcoal sketches, and black-and-white photographs. Fifty years and the musk of stale alcohol like a calling card and an invitation: welcome home.

As the door closes behind her, Lorrie slips the final piece of her ensemble in place: a black cat's eye mask that allows the other patrons to pretend they don't know her.

If you're of a certain age, the scene might make you think of Tommy Boy's[31] "Fat Guy in a Little Coat"[32] clip, except it's much, much worse than that. When Big Tub[33] settles his 450-pound frame in the hot tub, you expect that much mass to sink—Fat Guy in Little Swim Trunks—but all that adipose tissue, it floats. His batwings and his love handles (three handles per side, stacked like folding curls of thick custard) rise briefly on the bubbles. He's a big tub in a big tub so I call him Big Tub.

For awhile he lays facing the side wall, his ham hock arms crossed on the ledge beneath a not-unattractive face. The full force of a water jet pummeling his ponderous stomach. Me, I wonder if he can feel it: the pressure vibrating against his internal organs, making him just a wee bit nauseous between the sensation and the heat, and I think about what the jets might be pressure-washing from under his folds, like a woman with double-H breasts who never bothers to lift and clean until the sores develop. Accumulated sweat and dirt and bacteria build up there, begin eating the body from the outside-in, and with flesh bits maybe floating in the communal hot tub I reckon I should probably get out. Really what I reckon is that Big Tub should never have had the balls to get in, to even show that much skin, what must be miles of it, in a public place, in a gym where just by being present a thousand other toned bodies silently fat-shame him. In my mind I will him to get too hot, too red-faced, and evacuate, go have a lie-down on the nasty gray-tiled locker room floor.

As if my telepathic entreaty actually works, Big Tub

---

31 A 1995 American road comedy film.

32 https://www.youtube.com/watch?v=ohz8_lafGwE.

33 A regular at the author's gym. Mid-30s. Balding. He didn't know he was being watched.

shoves himself away from the ledge and into a standing position, the full transition requiring much time, a great effort, and a moan barely audible over the bubbles and the mic-amped voice of the Aquacise instructor in the neighboring pool. Only when Big Tub shuffles forward finding a step, gripping the handrail, taking one forever-step up, do I see the complete man, the hippopotamus inside him fully on view as he emerges, dripping from the spa like some walrus-cum-siren. His distended belly hangs in layers so low they flap against whatever balls have enabled him to show himself in the first place.

I am reminded of a story. In this story, a very fat young man afraid he will have his v-card forver, enlists the kind graces of a decent-looking prostitute over the internet. She shows up to his hotel room, takes one look at him, and says, 'Honey, how do you expect me to get to that dick? Lift your belly up with a forklift?' When he starts to whimper, for this woman was truly his last resort, the sex worker feels bad. She kisses the tears from his also not-unattractive face and one can assume, gets right down to business kissing other parts of his body, for there is a lot of it and she doesn't have all night.

The point is that amputation of a specific nature, let's call it medical excision, becomes necessary when a formerly obese person suddenly loses a lot of weight, or has liposuction performed. Exercise and diet shrink the fat cells and lipo makes them go bye-bye entirely, but what you're left with is the casing for all that fat, the miles of skin that make up your flesh house. It isn't supple and doesn't snap back; it sleeps. An unwelcome parasite on a slimmed-down body, and it must go. Like Shakespeare's Shylock[34] demanding a pound of flesh in payment for

---

[34] A Venetian-Jewish moneylender and principal antagonist of *The Merchant of Venice*.

a debt, or Billy[35] the puppet collecting on said debt in some warped form of atonement.

They should have just asked Big Tub to donate. I'll do it next time I see him.

---

[35] Unlike most killers, Jigsaw (who operates Billy the puppet) never intends to kill his subjects; the purpose of his traps is to see if the subject has the will to live.

Throwing her shoulders back and smiling beneath the mask, **LORRIE** walks confidently across the room to the bar. She's barely considered the liquor selection when a voice near her ear whispers: "Two whiskeys, neat." It's a deep voice, confident as Lorrie's shoulders, and she shyly eyes the man in a matching black eye mask, his blonde hair flopping like Westley's.[36] Notes the old-fashioned hook that is his left hand. They make small talk, mostly about business—there are few things sexier than money—and once Lorrie ascertains that his sexiness and intelligence quotients are at least equivalent to, if not greater than her alcohol intake, she invites the man back for a singular night of pleasure.

At Lorrie's apartment, they fumble their way through the dark to her bedroom. Only then does the moment of truth come. Taking a large medical bandage from the drawer by her bedside, Lorrie asks the man to tie it as tightly around her upper left arm as he can. The man asks if she uses drugs. Lorrie says, "No," and nothing else, so he follows her lead and complies without another word. "You have 20 minutes," Lorrie says, once he finishes with the tourniquet.

"Until your boyfriend gets home?" he quips.

"No. 'Til I take over."

The man begins. Both of them still wear their masks, and it reduces their collective humanity. Lorrie senses, rather than sees, the growing heat of her arm, the restricted blood backed up turgid and hot to the touch.

[36] From the 1987 American film *The Princess Bride*.

They pause to take something. Lorrie swallows the pill without bothering to ask, as what's the worst that could happen? They're already having sex; he isn't going to roofie her. Besides, she likes the game of guessing the chemical based on the high it delivers. Cannabis rolls her like a mind-orgasm. Ecstasy sharpens features but makes their edges soft as fleece. LSD arrives like a lucid dream. Suddenly her lover sprouts antlers and his love-moans are the grunt of rutting. She doesn't prefer one over the other, and if it takes her mind off the pain in her bound arm, the solid pain that precedes the numbing nothingness, so much the better. Lorrie feels the masked man's mouth sucking at her carotid like he'd suck the blood right out of her. She giggles, then barks when he bites. Just a nip, a little love bite, but from the warmth of it she can tell he's drawn blood.

At the edge of her vision, Lorrie sees the cold metal suspended from an impossible height. It hovers, shimmers as though shivering in some nonexistent breeze, at what must be 200 feet above ground. Lorrie consoles herself that at such height, the aid of gravity will surely cause a clean cut. Then she wonders, *Will it also affect the accuracy? How does one line up a limb with a blade that far away? It's simple physics*, Lorrie comforts herself again. If a diver can dive from a 75-meter board and hit the mark in a tiny pool every time, she can be-arm herself. Is that what it's called? Taking a guillotine not to the head, but the elbow?

In the school bathroom, **GEORGE** shakes his head. **SARAH**'s passing had felt like a guillotine to the heart, and some days he is sure the blade is still lodged there. Sarah was the only one who'd known his secret: that he believes, 100% and without a speck of doubt, that the body he lives in is not his own. You hear about white babies getting switched at the hospital, two sets of parents taking the wrong kid home. George thinks maybe his soul was switched to the wrong body at the last second, just before the goddess brought him down to be born. When he looks at himself in a mirror, he thinks maybe he only recognizes the eyes. Green with flecks of gold: a coyote's eyes. But that nose? It doesn't fit right. The air smells off when he breathes through it. How George can know this, he isn't sure, since it is quite the same nose he's always had, breathing the same Canyon de Chelly air he's always breathed.

But his nose is wrong.

His nose is wrong like his fingernails are wrong, from their mooney nail beds to the faint ridges decorating their surface. His nails are wrong like his feet are wrong: too flat instead of gracefully arched. He's always had trouble running on his toes. His feet are wrong like his ears are wrong, with their elephantine flare instead of the pointed, alert ears he knows he should have.

Those ears though. With their infernal ringing. The ringing exploding like a fire hydrant inside his head, all that pressurized water and no way to drain it. Sometimes George imagines that if he tips his head and shakes it just right, a dog's slobber-slinging shake, a flood might gush from out the extra-large lobes, then slow to a trickle, then cease. Taking with it the ringing.

TRICE pays the nominal fee for a guest pass and follows his client into the gym. The boy, **FOREST**, is 19 and already a veteran, having returned from his first deployment after just two months and short an entire right arm. The boy's body ends on his right side with an empty shoulder socket that dips into a badly-scarred armpit, scars that lash and braid together like briars down across his ribs and torso and stop mercifully short of his manhood. Forest looks over his other shoulder, his intact left side, to make sure Trice is following. Trice is, wishing he'd thought to wear anything other than the black suit that marks him as a fed. When on federal business, however...

Trice settles for loosening his tie and taking a spotting position above Forest, now scooching onto the weight bench on his back. Forest grips the bar with his good left hand and Trice grabs the press bar on the opposite side, assisting Forest as he completes his first bench press since "the accident." He watches Forest's chest muscles bulge with the effort, muscles he'd maintained by mastering one-handed push-ups. He can't bench unassisted though, and that is Trice's job: to create the custom prosthetic that will allow a transhumeral amputee to lift weights again, even to shoot a gun again. Forest, for his part, has every intention of returning to the Middle East.

With the eye of an engineer-artist, Trice memorizes the way that Forest's left elbow bends, the angle of his wrist, the strength with which his five fingers guide the bar methodically. He notes how the prosthesis will require an almost liquid-smooth mobility, and where it will need triple-reinforced. Not all amputees continue lifting weights, so it is an adaptation he will specially create for Forest Killian—his son.

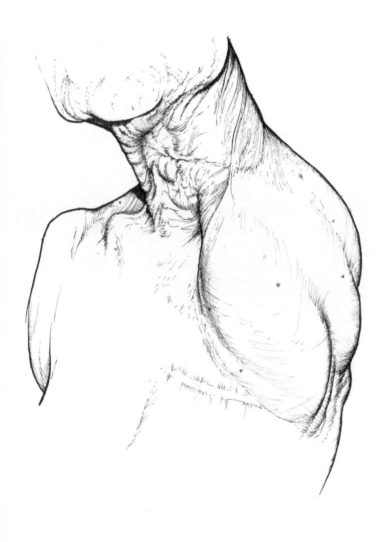

Whatever **LORRIE** takes, it is hallucinogenic. She knows that much. From behind her masked lover steps a beautiful woman, her long peroxide ponytail secured severely at the back of her head. (Even pulled up, the hair falls to her waist). The mystery woman wears a black leather corset that pushes her full breasts up roundly, a matching black g-string, gartered fishnets, and she carries a wooden paddle. Lorrie doesn't know where the woman has come from, but she thinks she couldn't imagine a sexier, more perfect creature. When **HANNAH** tells her to get on all fours, Lorrie complies with a grin. "And wipe that smile off your face!" Hannah commands. "Yes, mistress," Lorrie apologizes.

The things that Hannah, **BARTHOLOMEW**, and Lorrie do to each other for the next two hours are obscene and not the point of this book.

Lorrie awakes near dawn, when someone sneaks a warm hand between her legs, touching her just the way she likes. She shifts to give the hand better access, then realizes there is no one else in the room. The stranger's hand is her own, recently unbound and just starting to tingle as blood begins recirculating through the limb. As of yet, her arm still feels disconnected, like it isn't her own, and the moment feels disconnected, like she isn't alive, is in some predawn purgatory, waiting for morning to come, waiting to come.

CAPTAIN HOOK sits in the hot tub at the gym, his eyes closed, 104-degree water bubbling up to his shoulders, then just under his chin, as he sinks.relaxes. forgets. There'd been no water in the desert to speak of, no provincial ponds or fantastic oases. The tribal people had centuries ago learned to track plants and animals to underground springs, to harvest water from cacti and store it like camels. They'd learned to wrap their long hair in turbans against the sun and its heat, wrap their long legs in linen against the sand. They called the fashion Sunni and Shiite,[37] and created a whole religion around it. Or did the religion come first? Did Mother Mary wear a blue habit, or did the nuns co-opt the look after the fact? Either way, he's never forgotten the names. Sunni was like sunny, and all Afghanistan had was blasted sun. Shiite was like shit—the way the latrines perpetually smelled. He thanked bearded Allah that captains were exempt from latrine duty.

Because the water holds for Captain Hook no associations with the war, he loves it and he loves hot water especially, moving water, water with bubbles that obscure his stump. He tricks people that way, baiting them into arguments on morality and social justice, and when the war eventually comes up, he plays to or against their sympathies, offering calm argument after counter-argument, while his opponent, unaware, gets rather heated (and not just by the water). Bartholomew always lets them think they've had the last word. He bows his head, conciliatory and humble, then stands up, pulling the trailing fingers of his right hand from the water last of all, and when the unwitting victim sees that the Captain has no left arm at all, they grow

---

37 The two major denominations of Islam.

red (and not just from the water) and splutter (like their head is underwater) and the Captain walks away, and he is smiling.

It is disgraceful; and who can watch it but who can look away from the match that pits disabled against disabled.

From one dojo, a student with one arm. From a rival dojo, a blind master. One is young and one is wise and though both are outwardly crippled, their remaining muscles and other senses compensate, even give advantage to, their wounded warrior souls.

"Dad took a flashlight outside with him," GEORGE continues. "It was pitch black, not a single street lamp for miles to aid his night-sight, and if there was someone on the roof, he was determined to find him. There wasn't a tree for miles either, and the only ladder Dad found right where he always kept it, mounted on an interior garage wall. He opened and positioned the ladder against the front of the house, then climbed—steeled to see a large bird with clacking talons, or perhaps a dying prey animal dropped on the roof by said bird. Forget the fact that it'd sounded so totally like human feet. They hadn't even had a visitor since the previous fall. No one–" and nothing, George is tempted to add, "ever stopped for the night at the forlorn edge of the canyon."

"So what did he find?" an impatient student prompts George.

"Why, a man," George says.

The whole class looks at him suspiciously. "Or something man-like, anyway. His whole body, utterly naked, was painted in white clay, and his long hair fluttered like feathers from his wooden staff. My dad almost fell off the ladder, he was so frightened. But he managed to ask the man who he was and what he wanted—first in English, and then in Navajo. When the man would not respond, and my dad had started to question whether or not he was actually feeble-minded, he called the sheriff.

"The sheriff showed up with a deputy and two shotguns, and maybe because he finally had a worthy audience, the man on the roof spoke. 'I am a SKINWALKER,' he said, affirming the superstitious sheriff's worst fears. 'I've only now flown in from the desert.' Skinwalker or no, the man was very much a man. They led him gently down from the roof, clapped him in the backseat of the squad car, and my mom and dad at least never heard from him again."

"Do you think he was a skinwalker?" one student wants to know.

George pauses. He knows the man to be a skinwalker, but such proof as he has will only serve to make himself seem feeble-minded, too. George chooses another tactic. "It's not so important whether the skinwalker mythos is, in the true sense of the word, real. Rather, it parallels the Navajo narrative: a people who have been forced to assume many skins because of the color of our skin. We are brown like the soil, and copper as a vein of precious metal. We are creased by and created for the wind and the water and the sun, our cardinal brothers. Like the sun and the skinwalker, we shapeshift from night to day, from year to year, from ancient culture to a whitewashed approximation of culture. We blend in when we need to, knowing the secrets of camouflage, but stand proud when we ought to, the crow and the coyote to our left and our right. Industry and cunning, nest-builders and den-dwellers, with the impermanent mark of the Navajo, whose footprints blow away in the wind, but whose song is carried upward and forever by that same wind."

George suddenly realizes he's gotten lost in his own language. He surveys the class, some of whom he's likewise lost, and not to anything like rapture.

"We're going to do a writing assignment," George tells them. "Take out a pen and paper."

CAPTAIN HOOK eyes the slide at 100x magnification, adjusting the fine focus until 5 blistered cells come cleanly into view. The slide holds a preserved sample of his edge-skin, cut from the place where arm falls away to empty space. They had to test the skin, they told him, for residual gunpowder, so they knew whose bomb it was that'd claimed his non-dominant hand: ours or the enemy's. "Sure," Bartholomew remembers saying. "Take it." Still dazed then over his newfound carnal knowledge. When the surgeon closed up the wound, borrowing skin flaps from his back like denim patches, Bartholomew was unconscious—or he would have told the doctor he was doing it wrong. The surgeon, he left just a nubbin too much of cartilage and bone beneath the human flesh bandage. "Hand me that file," Bartholomew would have said. "Let me show you, dear doctor, how it's done." Gritting his teeth, he would have, he swears, filed that raw and bleeding bone right down to its proper proportions—the point where his arm was supposed to end. He knew that spot like the freckles on his gone and lost forearm—a limb that never should have been there in the first place, but from which he was now gloriously liberated.

Bartholomew studies the cells through the viewfinder, looks at their frozen, inanimate lines. The way each cell's dark nucleus hangs suspended in a whole lot of negative space, save for the mitochondria spiraling out like mini umbilical cords. The brain of the cell and the powerhouse of the cell and none of those cells smart enough to do what needs doing. He will fix that, though, his nubbin—and then fix those who also need fixing.

He turns to the lab rats running on their wheels, running and running, as he thought he had, away from danger, never realizing that it was in the direction of salvation they all needed to run.

Saturday night, **LORRIE** stays in and watches a movie with her black cats Sibyl and Stella. Her left arm bears all the signs of strangulation, with a deep red bruise like a cilice, and her brain feels as if it, too, has been strangled, quite unrecovered from whatever pills they'd taken.

Her masked lover. She doesn't even know his name.

Lorrie grins. She likes it that way. Her sexy skinwalker. He could come (and come, and come again) and go as he pleased. On both him and his hallucinogenic medicine, she is hooked.

UMI was a woman before she was a boy-child, who at 30 should be called a man but for the teenage acne and absence of any tits at all, even the kind that obese little boys get. The acne is from the hormone injections and the titless chest was spawned the day that Umi had both breasts and two nipples amputated. Cause of breast death: body dysmorphic disorder.[38] The diagnosis allows doctors to sever healthy flesh for medically-unnecessary reasons. No one can argue with the psyche because no one really understands it. We have theories, not facts. The standard model of particle physics was a theory until the Large Hadron Collider[39] at CERN actually found a Higgs Boson. And it's still just a theory.

But if parts and pieces can be removed for BDD, BIID is just a step away. Then doctors won't be disbarred for malpractice and wannabes won't inject themselves, pierce themselves, trying to become what they were born to be.

---

[38] Characterized by an obsessive preoccupation with some aspect of one's own appearance, in which a perceived flaw warrants exceptional measures to hide or fix it.

[39] The world's largest and most powerful particle collider, most complex experimental facility ever built, and the largest single machine in the world.

FOREST, TRICE's only and illegitimate son, was not, thankfully, the product of his unions with the First Lady. Contrary to popular belief, the president of the United States does not actually make that much money, not compared to a corporate CEO anyway. It wouldn't have been worth blackmailing the First Family, and Trice couldn't have done that to her anyway. He'd taken her in enough unromantic broom closets that she didn't need public ignominy piled on top of it all.

No, Forest sprang from **VICKI**'s womb, the cute girl who used to show for Guillotine games at the comic book shop. Trice thinks that is probably most of the reason that at age 39 he still attends—to feel close to her. He'd loved her and he should have married her, but he never knew about Forest until Vicki called him one night crying, saying his son had been wounded in war and did he, Trice, want to meet them at the VA clinic in Washington, DC? "Of course!" Trice had said, responding more to the panic in her voice than the new knowledge of his offspring. He'd cabbed to the VA clinic immediately, asked for Vicki at the desk, and had been shown to a room where his sometime-lover lay silently weeping upon the chest of a boy who was undoubtedly, even at first glance, his. Forest's skin was that particularly rich shade of chocolate common to the mixing of a Kenyan father and an Irish mother, Vicki the cream in the morning coffee he'd never shared with her again.

Trice had surveyed the damage, noting the missing arm immediately. Even though a white blanket had been pulled up to Forest's chin, the telltale dip where a body should continue was obvious in its lack. He'd gripped Vicki's shaking shoulders and kissed the middle of her back, before taking a seat beside her for the duration of her vigil. Trice had demanded exactly as many answers that night as Vicki willingly offered: absolutely none. Instead he'd gazed upon his son with all the intensity of 18 years, trying to fill in memories he'd never made. Imagining what Forest must have looked like as an infant—and Vicki, delivering him. Had she been alone? He'd marveled at her strength. Before that night, they hadn't spoken in years.

Trice watches, lost in thought, as a 3D printer deposits precise layers of green silicone. The silicone is the color and consistency of slime until it solidifies into flexible, heat-resistant fibers, durable over years of consistent use.

Sunday night, at 11:55 PM, **CAPTAIN HOOK** tweets the link to a buried webpage. Stark, with a black background and gold text, the page hints at mystery and luxury and madness. It calls for volunteers to audition for a new show called "Church" to be held at an underground art space in Chicago. Auditions take place every night at midnight; the show is scheduled for the following week. Lorrie sees the link when a Chicago friend retweets it. Lorrie clicks the link. Lorrie reads.

In 2014, Hollywood actor Ryan Gosling[40] premiered his directorial debut, *Lost River*, at Austin's SXSW[41] music, film, and tech fest. The story of a single mother with 2 sons to support, *Lost River* traces Mom's employment at a singular kind of burlesque club, where the "slicing," "stabbing," and "cutting" of the dancers, either by other dancers or the clientele acting out their darkest fantasies, is the feature presentation. It's supposed to be fake, really excellent movie magic, like when Mom outlines her pretty face with a scalpel, then pulls the bloody visage away. And it is fake—until, of course, things go too far. This is amputation for art's sake, for pleasure, for paying patrons.

This is show business.

---

[40] Canadian actor and musician, b. 1980.

[41] South by Southwest, b. 1987.

It's weird, right, that frostbite is a thing? Like, we deepfreeze animal meat all the time, then thaw it and eat it and call it perfectly healthy, some "lean protein" for a balanced diet. Why, then, is human flesh unsalvageable once it's frozen? Why do toes turn black and threaten to rot off, making amputation the prescription?

Why is cutting off the affected part still the standard cure? How come the BRCA[42] gene forces celebs like Angelina Jolie[43] to preemptively undergo a double mastectomy? Maybe she had inverted nipples and the procedure was partly cosmetic? Decease your risk of cancer, increase your bust size? You can't dose with chemo or irradiate cancer that isn't there yet and which may never develop. But you can cut off the bad part, the undesirable part, like a mole or a skin tag or a wart. You can say, *This is no longer a part of me.* Or if you have BIID, you can say, *This never was a part of me.*

---

[42] The "breast cancer susceptibility" gene and its attendant protein.

[43] American actress, filmmaker, and humanitarian.

I ask him what he knows about amputation. "I know more about amputation then than amputation now," he says.

"Okay."

"Then, they gave you a whiskey shot and cut in at an angle, so they could fold the skin and muscle flap over and whipstitch it like a dolphin wing."

"A dolphin wing."

"I also know it hurt like a sonofabitch."

One eyebrow cocked, I look him up and down. "Do you have a prosthetic limb I should know about?"

He laughs. "Don't worry about it."

Sometimes the present grows like a wall around the fragile remnants of the past. One minute you're walking down Michigan Ave.,[44] modern retail and contemporary restaurants as far as the eye can see, couture and cuisine, black protestors picketing the death of another black teen by another white cop in this high-end area for maximum exposure. The next, you're facing a two-hundred-year-old church, its white brick crumbling but its alcoves kept cobweb-free by a dedicated team of preservation specialists. Historic Sites is another department under the same state government umbrella as **LORRIE**'s museum. The church is one, but the bunker-turned-club in the middle of the meatpacking district? If it is on any official's radar, certainly it hadn't been on Lorrie's.

She supposes it makes sense. Factory workers during the war would themselves have needed a safe space to hide in the event of an air raid on their munitions manufacturing facilities.

Once inside the space, Lorrie can see that the bunker has been just a little bit altered since its days as a public welfare and weapons conservatory. For one thing, a round oculus has been cut into the stone ceiling, letting in both the snow and the chill night air. Directly beneath the hole, however, blazes a giant bonfire, kept constantly stoked by four blonde women in neck-to-toe black leather catsuits. The have neat piles of logs and iron pokers at the ready and like the fuzzy British police they take their work seriously.

Next Lorrie notices how sluices cut into the slab floor circulate superheated water from underneath the fire pit to four concrete pools at each corner. Men and women and people of no gender at all lounge in the pools or

---

[44] A major north-south street in Chicago, also known as the Magnificent Mile.

dangle toes in from the edge. Many of them are naked and not everyone is classically attractive—but they wear their confidence like A-list clothing and it is redemptive, in a nearly Biblical sense. *Enter my waters and be made new*, Lorrie thinks, and smiles at her own silliness within the scene's larger absurdity.

She spots the bar against the back wall and heads toward it, her high heels clicking proudly. The confidence that oozes through the room like a syrup does not discriminate, and Lorrie is happy to realize she belongs. Others look her up and down as she crosses the room and Lorrie wonders if she'll meet someone. She wonders who among them is there to be taught, and who to do the teaching.

Strong cocktail in hand, she finds a table by what seems to be the stage: a raised platform set up between two pools at the far end. She sits and sips and she waits for the show to begin.

Zozobra[45] is the papier-mâché doll's name. In New Mexico, they build him every year and then set him on fire along with thousands of handwritten notes—secrets and confessions and regrets—harbored from the past year and wiped clean with the New Year. The largest Zozobra ever constructed stood 50.17 feet tall and took only minutes to burn. You can watch YouTube videos of the spectacle, the doll's mouth opening and closing to belch out bursts of flame, its whole body alight from the inside. Scaffolding depicted in X-ray. The Zozo's eyes don't open and close and somehow that makes it worse. Like Zoltar,[46] he sees all—every pencil-scratched prayer—and he pays for your sins.

Two states away, **GEORGE** is not unfamiliar with the Zozobra concept. The Navajo have their own totemic objects to be imbued with power, used as tools to harness power, or to render another person powerless. Such are the fetishes of shamans and holy men—like the one who stands over George now.

---

[45] A giant marionette effigy built and burned every autumn during Fiestas de Santa Fe in Santa Fe, New Mexico.

[46] An antique arcade fortune telling machine.

"I am what is sometimes known as a 'qualia freak.' I think that there are certain features of the bodily sensations especially, but also of certain perceptual experiences, which no amount of purely physical information includes. Tell me everything physical there is to tell about what is going on in a living brain, the kind of states, their functional role, their relation to what goes on at other times and in other brains, and so on and so forth, and be I as clever as can be in fitting it all together, you won't have told me about the hurtfulness of pains, the itchiness of itches, pangs of jealousy, or about the characteristic experience of tasting a lemon, smelling a rose, hearing a loud noise, or seeing the sky."

—FRANK JACKSON, "THE QUALIA PROBLEM"[47]

[47] Australian analytic philosopher, currently Distinguished Professor and former Director of the Research School of Social Science at Australian National University.

Google "German cannibal" and all links lead to Meiwes.[48] If the consumption of human flesh does a cannibal make, Meiwes was in every sense of the word a cannibal. Today he's serving a prison sentence for manslaughter—not murder—because while his meal died as a direct result of blood loss from injuries inflicted by Meiwes to one Bernd Jürgen Armando Brandes, the death was not a homicide. If mutual consent does an assisted suicide make—and euthanasia is legal in Germany—then Brandes died willingly and Miewes is not a killer in the cold-blooded sense.

It went like this: Forty-year-old Miewes placed an internet ad on a cannibal fetish site for a 'well-built male' who wanted to be killed and eaten. When Brandes responded, Miewes interviewed him several times on video. On the day of the deed, Miewes plied Brandes with alcohol and aspirin at his request. Miewes then amputated Brandes's penis. Both men attempted to share it raw, but found the muscle too 'chewy' for their liking. Miewes went to fry it with flour and pepper; meanwhile, Brandes lost consciousness. Some time later, Miewes pronounced Brandes dead, finished dismembering him, and 'packaged' the meat in his freezer. He would eat 44 pounds of Brandes over the next 10 months. Consuming the flesh gave Miewes self-described sexual gratification.

Miewes was 'caught' when he described Brandes's demise on the same fetish site and asked for another volunteer. A concerned reader turned the cops onto the case. Miewes was only convicted following a forced appeal initiated by prosecutors.

At time of writing, the video footage of the act has not been released.

---

[48] A German computer repair technician who achieved international notoriety for killing and eating a coluntary victim whom he had found via the Internet.

The show can only happen once at this location, with these clients, using these props. It's Roswell[49] with the aliens and Pennsylvania with flight number 93[50] and every other "conspiracy" that happened once and never again, never to be solved or atoned for or even believed the following morning when dawn evaporates the nightmare's power and any certainty that things directly experienced were never real at all.

LORRIE sits so close to the action that she'll later recall the sword gleaming above her own head, foresight glinting off its polished steel point. An ancient and ritualized amputation starts the ceremony. **CAPTAIN HOOK**'s science fiction creations cap it. Only when he takes the stage does Lorrie realize with whom she slept.

The penultimate exhibit begins with a delicate surgery. Bartholomew, having acquired a passable dexterity with his prosthetic hand, slips a sterile scalpel just through the surface of a young woman's tissue-thin wrist flesh. The procedure is reflected in and magnified by a canted mirror suspended above the stage. Lorrie sees blood well like a thick licorice stripe across the length of the incision. Bartholomew's assistant uses forceps to pull the cut apart, and into her wrist Bartholomew inserts a .5" niobium cube. Onstage, the woman grimaces but does not squirm. The sweat speckling her brow might be from the pain, the audience's scrutiny, or profound anticipation and arousal. Lorrie can commiserate. She's been dreaming more vividly of late.

Once Captain Hook's cube is tucked securely in place, he drapes the woman's arm with a weighted flak jacket—the kind they pass out to American kiddos during school

---

[49] A city in New Mexico known for the Roswell UFO Incident (1947).

[50] A domestic passenger flight hijacked by four Al-Qaeda terrorists on board, as part of the September 11 attacks.

shootings (routine now as tornado drills). Satisfied, he steps away, trailing his fingers along the woman's chin— she is quite beautiful. As he does so, he turns her own head away from the sight, reassuring her with a surgeon's smile.

"Three," he breathes, not bothering to count the one and the two. Captain Hook's finger depresses the remote detonator. The woman's left arm vaporizes with a quiet puff and the slightest jump of the shrapnel guard. Tears stream from her eyes but they look nothing like a sinner's and everything like one reborn. As her mutilation was not itself the draw, but rather her redemption, Bartholomew does not lift the blanket for the crowd to ogle. Wrapping it gently around her raw stump, he escorts the woman offstage, blood blooming across the surface of the bullet-proof fabric. It saturates but does not drip.

Finally it is the Captain's turn. Taking centerstage again, he prepares like an athlete, martial artist, or big shot CEO: he visualizes his success from beginning to bloody end. He promises himself the reward of a lifetime. No government-issued, president-pinned Purple Heart[51] can compare to emerging one day shy of 31, newly-bodied. Abs hard, prick hard, striated scar tissue marking where Captain Bartholomew Jordan (properly this time) becomes Captain Hook.

---

[51] A United States military decoration awarded in the name of the President to those wounded or killed while serving in the U.S. military.

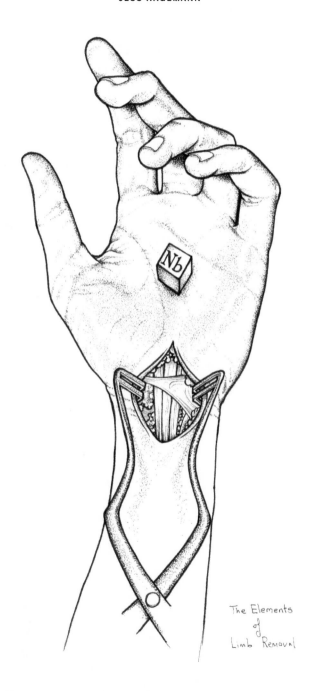

The Elements
of
Limb Removal

With the push of a computer key, **TRICE** directs Lab 042's twelfth 3D printer to begin to build from tiny layers of carbon fiber composite a brand new index finger for his son, army veteran **FOREST**.

The finger must integrate form and function, must lift weights, grip a coffee cup, must trace a someday-girlfriend's soft hip hollows, must hoist and catch their hypothetical children. Trice's grandchildren. Must attract attention but never pity—in the streets start conversations, not the condescension of disability.

Trice authorizes the next processor: PLA[52] pours from metal spigots, hard plastic molten but cooling instantly on contact with the stainless steel base. Trice smiles. For two weeks he's been the father of an 18-year-old man. For the first time, his work is personal. Imbued with the greatest purpose there is.

---

[52] PolyLactic Acid, a biodegradable biopolymer.

Bethany Hamilton[53] fed her arm to a shark in Kauai. In the middle of a surfing competition. On live TV. Afterward, God told her to be strong.

LORRIE likes to go in the hot tub on her period. According to a campy tampon commercial from Russia, doing so attracts sharks. If sharks lived in a hot tub.

Today there is one. An old black shark who sits curled up in the corner, his arm moving spastically. When Lorrie realizes he's jacking off underwater, she blanches in disgust. But then remembers the brew the two of them are making. Semen and blood, blood and semen. Thinks maybe this was the primordial ooze. Father Time's spunk, Mother Earth's monthly.

---

[53] An American professional surfer who survived a 2003 shark attack.

While we tear each other apart, the starfish are offing themselves, arms twisting and crawling, stretching away toward—nothing but death. The stretch becoming a tiny tear, a maddening rip, liquids spilling like blue blood into a bluer sea. They get the lesions first, round patches of fuzzy white, spoiled kale left too long in the fridge, forgotten.

"The feature of the salamander that attracts most attention is its healing ability: the axolotl does not heal by scarring and is capable of the regeneration of entire lost appendages in a period of months, and, in certain cases, more vital structures. Some have indeed been found restoring the less vital parts of their brains. They can also readily accept transplants from other individuals, including eyes and parts of the brain—restoring these alien organs to full functionality. In some cases, axolotls have been known to repair a damaged limb, as well as regenerating an additional one, ending up with an extra appendage that makes them attractive to pet owners as a novelty. In metamorphosed individuals, however, the ability to regenerate is greatly diminished. The axolotl is therefore used as a model for the development of limbs in vertebrates."
—WIKIPEDIA

For a week, **LORRIE** ponders the things she saw in Chicago, in some for-one-night-only converted bunker. She yearns for the touch of the man from the bar whose name she doesn't know—the same stunning man who choreographed Church—and the wonderful woman who lived inside their hallucination. When she can stand it no longer, Lorrie finagles a beach vacation out of a courier trip to San Diego, better even than Miami.

The University of California at San Diego houses a Pacific Rim collection on what would take up eight miles of shelving units set end to end, but store rather compactly in a couple large rooms underground. For its next magic trick, the museum has planned an interactive exhibit on President Obama's Trans-Pacific Partnership.[54] Smart screens will update the content in real time while static displays will showcase relics from each of the twelve participating countries' indigenous people—those whom the TPP was in part designed to assist. From UCSD Lorrie is to escort a set of Malaysian stone tools, embedded in a 1.8 million-year-old meteorite, a Singaporean Komodo dragon skeleton, and a Kiwi flax purse.

Because the Monday of her scheduled meeting falls on a state holiday, Lorrie is able to extend the trip by the weekend before and an extra Tuesday. She takes a room in the Gaslamp Quarter[55] and spends long days on the coast, cradled in Ocean Beach's sandy hillocks with a bottle of water or a Long Island Iced Tea, lulled and mesmerized by the ceaseless waves and the just-hot sun pricking her bare legs whenever the breeze slows. She spends equally long nights indulging the Gaslamp's gourmet food scene: a trio of bellinis paired with cajun avocado fries. Sashimi

[54] A trade agreement between Australia, Brunei, Canada, Chile, Japan, Malaysia, Mexico, New Zealand, Peru, Singapore, the United States (until January 23, 2017) and Vietnam.

[55] The historic heart of San Diego.

so fresh it makes the sake sing on her tongue.

San Diego is a beautiful town full of beautiful people. On Monday evening at the hotel bar, understatedly-beautiful Lorrie attracts her own attention. It's early yet, and the first shift bartender is just finishing up. Lorrie'd been one of two customers that **QUINN** had served that afternoon, and he admires the woman's taste. Black jeans, boots, and a black low-cut tank top. Her black leather jacket hangs from the stool's shoulders. Her drink requests had been similarly neat. For hours she had sipped and stared at the sunlight through the windows, how it danced at increasingly acute angles the lower that skysphere sank. She hadn't spoken except to order, though Quinn had noticed that she doodled sometimes absentmindedly on a bar napkin.

When Quinn cashes out, handing the reins to his second-shift replacement, he approaches Lorrie's end of the bar.

"Can I take you to dinner?"

If she hears him, it takes a second to register. Lorrie's eyes blink rapidly like she is returning after some deep space travel. She remembers to smile, then tells him that she already has a reservation at the Prado.

"But I can make it for two," she offers.

Quinn drives.

It becomes the kind of red wine night that makes Lorrie feel warm, cocooned, and overly friendly with a man she's only just met. The night wraps around her like his arms do later, and wherein two consenting adults know there will not be a future, and also that it doesn't matter, not really, not if the world ends tonight anyway, when Quinn asks Lorrie, "Where to?" after their date, she says simply, "Inside me"—distracted once more by the sky.

Pulling into Quinn's driveway, Lorrie looks at the condo blankly, then exits the car and walks up to the door as if she's been there many times before. She picks her way around furniture and in the dark leads them both upstairs to Quinn's loft room, where the stars blaze through the skylight like diamonds.

Quinn follows her silently. Curious and turned on.

Lorrie sits on the bed, facing him, Quinn's belly at eye level, her fingers finding purchase immediately at Quinn's belt. She seems driven by some purpose beyond just getting him "inside her." When she sees it, her breath sucks in a tiny audible bit. Quinn is surprised. He'd thought he'd mastered the limp long ago, that no one on the outside could tell. But Lorrie falls to unbuckling his prosthetic leg with the same concentration she'd applied to his belt, and a smile creases Quinn's lips in the dark. This woman is something else.

Some days **ANNA** hates the world. From the stupid city she lives in, with its idiot residents, to the stupid school she'd thought she'd been escaping to, with its students so idiotic she wonders if Stanton has any admissions standards at all. Anna hates feeling 'above' everybody while longing so desperately for a single sympathetic soul to look her way. Aware of the irony that arrogance repels more than it attracts the perfect Other, she nevertheless tries to believe that if she exists, he must, too. Or she. Anna is pansexual and so non-discriminating on every quality other than basic intelligence and self-awareness that she should be much more likely to have a boyfriend than her bigoted, homophobic, fundamentalist roommate K.—and yet, K. is the one now dating Stanton's starting quarterback. And K. isn't even that pretty! Okay, maybe in the traditional sense, all blonde and busty. But not interesting to look at, like Anna with her asymmetrical earrings, fashionably mismatched clothes, and her two white hands at the ends of her otherwise very Asian wrists.

Bones. Tendons. Arteries. Nerves. Veins. Skin.

This had been the order that the surgeon sewed donor hand to recipient body, after Anna lost her own hands to a duel with a firecracker. She calls it a duel because it's kind of a joke and you laugh at jokes and when you're laughing it's harder to cry. So Anna describes the way they chose their weapons: fist vs. gunpowder; and how neither really challenged the other. It was N. who'd drunkenly suggested the whole thing. Told her to take the cherry bomb to the end of the dock, strike a match, and run away. It wasn't really just her fist she'd been fighting with but also firepower and two strong legs that looked good that summer, all July-tan after a month spent visiting relatives in the Ozarks, and waterskiing from the back of their boat every day. All these parts combined, however, had been no match for a lit match held to the end of a too-quick wick. Before Anna could even uncrouch, her hands had been returned to the dust from which they came: albeit in red chunks and shards of bone. Only the reflex of a blink saved her eyes. Brows and lashes and the baby fine fuzz of her soft face flash-fried to hairlessness.

K. had been there, too, and it was K. who'd thought to tie Anna's hoodie around her shortened arms, cinching the blood that (in as much shock, apparently, as Anna) had been slow to actually waterfall from Anna's open mouths. N. had looked on silently, maybe secretly wishing to black out, maybe secretly believing he already had. Some days later, he'd found part of Anna's pink-painted fingernail fallen into his own hoodie pocket.

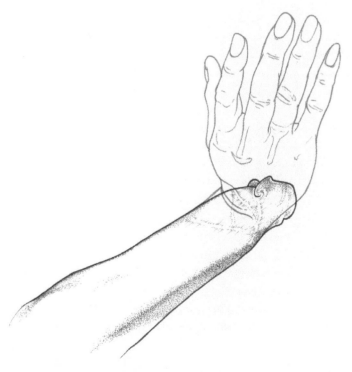

It's kind of the perfect solution, right? As advances continue in what's known as "solid organ" transplant (i.e. structures like the hand), people who don't want theirs anymore can just donate them to people who either never had the organ to begin with, or who lost it through some accident, freak or otherwise.

Anna's hands came from a braindead donor, the family giving their blessing if only to see their teenage daughter live on in some small way through someone else. In that case, the drunk driver had rendered unviable all of their daughter's internal organs (pieces of both cars' occupants decorated the windshields and the road) but her hands had survived without a scrape. The match had been confirmed (what a 'match' it was, Anna scoffed again, staring at her lily white hands, so glaringly different from her tan Thai skin) and Anna had been notified right away. It was a moment she'd been preparing for in some non-real way since her doctor had identified her as a suitable candidate for transplantation. But really? How did one just drop everything and get ready to undergo major surgery at the singing of a Kesha[56] ringtone?

And it was major: 8-12 hours major. She emerged more debilitated than she'd been while lacking two limbs. Weeks and months and years of rehab, left toes crossed that the fingers of her new right hand might somehow regenerate nerves that did anything more than cause phantom pains, but maybe actually move. After all, Anna'd learned to give a pretty mean handjob; so mean that most boys didn't even miss the blowjob.

Two years after the transplant, Anna can grip a pencil, though she's lost the beautiful Asian penmanship she once had. By the same token, she can grip a penis, and her unique situation doesn't seem to affect that skill too

[56] An American singer, songwriter, and rapper.

greatly at least. She has some feeling in the hands, too. A little. Sensitive more to temperature than pressure differences, Anna feels the heat of scalding water long before she senses its wetness. The hands feel a part of her (because they are) and also not (because they aren't).

Unwashed human has a very specific smell. Kind of earthy, though not in a pleasant way. Mother Earth gone sour, with just a hint of sweet rot. Having been around it most of his life, **FOREST** likens the aroma to spoiled carrot cake. Orange vegetable curls undecipherable from the orange mold growing in its once-moist cinnamon agar, the cream cheese icing now hard and flavorless as concrete, or curdled into syphilitic smegma.

What role do unwashed humans play in the ecosystem? How vital are the organisms that feed on them? Can we amputate one sector of the population, like warts from the genitals of a smiling dog?

XIOMARA celebrates her 101st birthday on January 8 by having her leg amputated from the knee down. The original blood clot operation was not successful, so they take the whole limb instead. Imagine waking up from surgery without the foot that'd carried you one year farther than an entire century. Imagine dying from the grief of loss—not when your husband died, but when the self you knew does.

The next time Xiomara wakes up after the time she didn't have a leg, she wakes up inside a dream of the purgatory her fire-and-brimstone father had taught her to fear. She isn't dirty enough for hell but she isn't clean enough for heaven, either. In this analogy, it'd be like finding oneself forever stuck in the gap between leg and not-leg: the empty air your hand bats through when you try to scratch the spot that always itched just on top of the tibia.

Xiomara never wakes up from the dream, and I can't tell you if she goes to heaven or not. This is not omniscient narration, but a record of how it was.

LORRIE meets **ANNA** at a club. Anna is celebrating her 21st birthday with bumping and grinding and too many tequila shots. Anna raises her empty glass and three fingers above the throng at the bar to signal the bartender "three more," and her apparent vitiligo catches Lorrie's eye. She's never seen such a perfect demarcation between hand and arm, a veritable line at the wrist like a scar-brace-let joining. Fusing. Lorries quickly runs through all the possible explanations. Self-mutilation. Accident. But what could have caused the bleaching of Anna's skin? Beautiful, exotic, obviously Asian Anna. Unless—

That Anna might have been the recipient of new hands, hands other than her own, is almost too difficult to grasp for a woman who daydreams about separating herself from herself. Then other ideas begin to form: hazy rum-punch notions of donating parts she doesn't need to someone who could use them. Like she is a character from *Never Let Me Go*,[57] born and bred just to grow parts for others. It gives Lorrie an odd sense of pride, this niggling seed of *what if*, and a thought for the first time that her deformity can in fact be somehow useful.

As red and yellow disco lights swim over the hybrid girl's body, Lorrie feels her own head swim and decides only another drink will set it right.

Lorrie watches as the bartender sets three wobble-full shots before Anna then waves her own white hand at the man. He's cute, she notices, though his arms aren't as built as the guy she was just dancing with. He'd been wearing a hoodie with the hood up. Not the most pretentious of club wear, but then his biceps pulled the terrycloth tight. She couldn't see his face, but the lights had danced on his eyes every so often with the same intensity with which

---

[57] A 2005 dystopian science fiction novel by Japanese-born British author Kazuo Ishiguro.

he'd danced—precise; controlled; an artist responding to her like a machine. Lorrie had let him dance with her because he'd made no move to grope her, only to act as her fluid shadow, sliding hips against hips without ever once touching, respecting her space but his desire evident in the way he also strained at the crotch of his jeans. Lorrie didn't know quite what to make of him, except for the fact that the greater the pains he took not to touch her, the more she desperately wanted him to. Parched, she'd gone to get a drink at the bar when she'd spotted Anna. Who knew if she'd find her suggestion of a lover again.

In the bathroom, Lorrie checks her eye makeup, applies more lipstain, squats above a toilet seat already saturated with piss. She checks to make sure there's still a condom in her purse, just in case. She flushes, wiping the seat off for the next woman, just because. Because it may be a club meant for booze and bad decisions, but goddammit a girl should be entitled to a clean public toilet even if its next occupant will throw up all the alcohol she just threw back, spotting seat and tank and miniskirt in the process.

Lorrie smiles at the women in line as she exits and she's still smiling when she looks up into his eyes. Mr. Almost-Lover. Her smile morphs into a self-conscious grin, into a tiny moan as **BARTHOLOMEW**'s strong right hand and stronger left hook finally grip her wrists, circling like scar-bracelets between hand and arm.

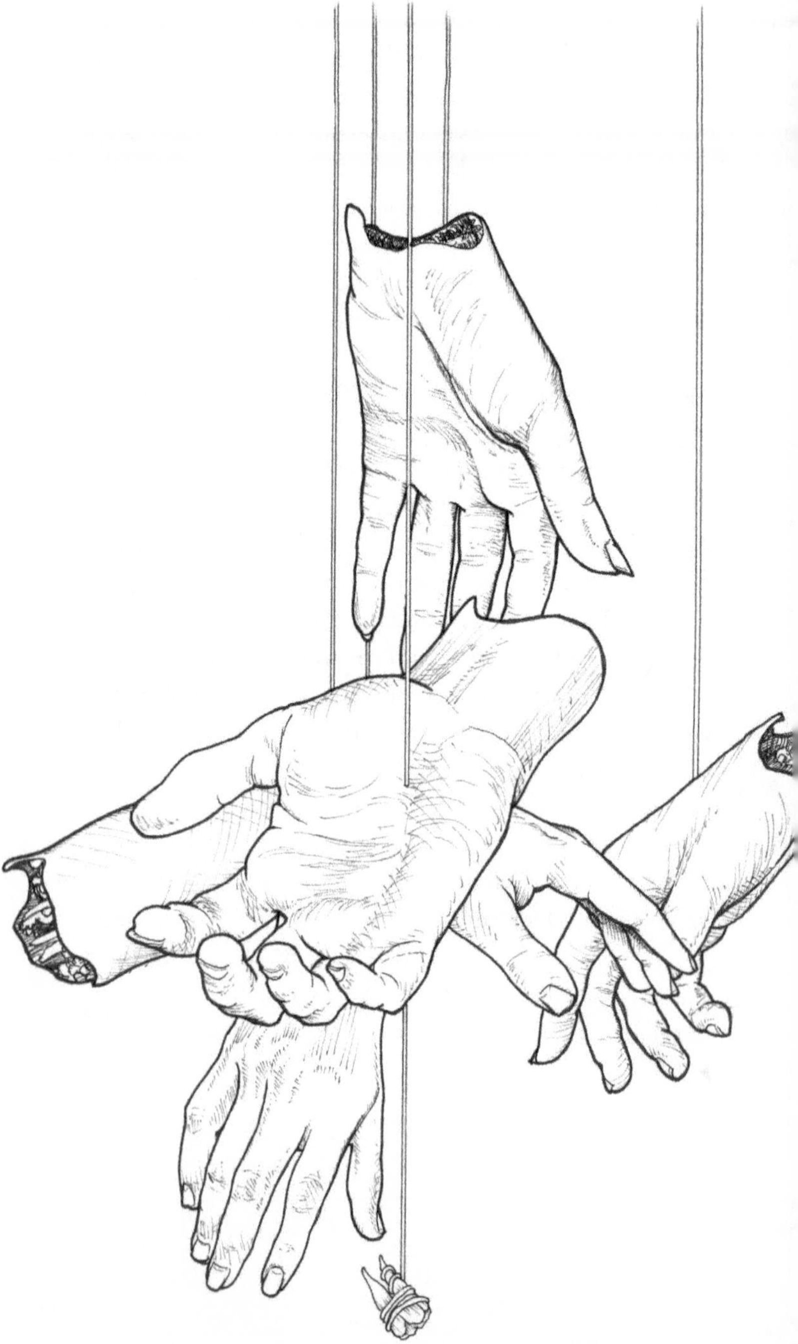

There's a special spot in Canyon de Chelly where **GEORGE** likes to go because the wind funnels and tunnels through the crevasses with such force that it howls, and when the very air is screaming his ears don't ring. Well, probably they still do, but he can't hear the cursed things for once and the respite is blessed.

Unlike B. B. cannot be blessed because yesterday he jumped from canyon top to bottom, and taking the life God gave you before God does is an unpardonable offense. B. had been panhandling at the four-way stop in town (it gets a lot of tourist traffic from blue-hairs headed to the casino) and his pockets were still full of loose paper and change when he jumped. Which is why George thinks that maybe he didn't jump.

CAPTAIN HOOK watched **LORRIE** at the bunker show in Chicago. He danced with her at a club two weeks later. On Thursday, Bartholomew, having done his due diligence, pulls up the barstool next to Lorrie's and doesn't say a thing. He doesn't order a drink or hit on his prize; just taps the metal knuckles of his fancy prosthetic arm (unlike any Lorrie has ever seen) against the beer-damp wooden counter and waits for Lorrie to look up from her phone. Tonight he will tell her that she is his.

IRA and **ELIOT** have only been together a little over a year and the sex is already boring.

One night Ira goes home with somebody else, learns a thing or two, and returns to Eliot ready to rekindle their last-gasp relationship. He knows what he needs now, he tells a dubious Eliot, who forgives Ira's transgression only because he's 'comfortable' and scared of starting over again. Especially when he's not yet 'out' to his family. Especially since Ira is his first true love. Eliot knows the sex is boring, but it's safe. Neither has any STDs (save for what Ira might've caught in a stranger's bed—though he swears they used condoms [multiple / Ira doesn't bother to hide the enthusiasm in his voice] because that stud was ready to go again just as soon as they'd finished—the implication being that he was unlike [and therefore better than] Eliot, who preferred cuddling to back-to-back bareback—not that he ever would've voiced such a thing to Ira).

Though he supposes that Ira knows it anyway and it's just one more thing for Ira to get fed up with. Grow tired of. Replace him over. Knowing all these things, Eliot merely meekly asks, "What do you want me to do?"

"Choke me," Ira says.

Asphyxiation is a fetish like any other, but that's not the kind of choking Ira means. He laughs derisively when Eliot gently puts his hands around his lover's neck as they fool around in bed later that night. "Not there," Ira says. "Here." He guides Eliot's hands down to his hard cock, confusing Eliot, who can't believe that his hardcore boyfriend, always too good for handjobs, would request such a thing now. Ira places Eliot's fingers in a tight little ring around the base of his penis, then tells him to squeeze—hard. "Harder!" he nearly yells. Ira's default coping mechanism is anger.

Eliot squeezes at about 50% of his maximum capability. No matter what Ira tells him, he isn't out to hurt his lover. "Now, when I'm about to come, I want you to squeeze, just like that but harder, you son of a bitch." Ira never speaks to Eliot endearingly and in fact has only once told him he loves him—while shitfaced at a New Year's Eve party. He'd later kissed someone else that same night. "Squeeze so hard I don't ejaculate," Ira continues. "Like a vice, get it? My splooge won't even get through, if you squeeze right."

"But you'll still orgasm?"

"Oh yeahhh," Ira says, grinning.

Eliot frowns. "What's the point?"

"One, it feels amazing. Two, it will force you to grow some balls and be a fucking man for once. Take some control; don't make me do all the work all the time."

This is news to Eliot. As the dominant one, Ira never wants anything more from his pussy sub than complacent obedience. Suck harder. Flip over. These are the commands that Eliot is used to hearing. Not 'Man up.' But if Ira is giving him a chance, Eliot will at least try. How hard can it be to choke a cock?

At 22, Eliot has a degree but no real direction other than what Ira tells him to do. He prefers taking orders to charting his own course—and it isn't a matter of laziness. If Eliot thought Ira could love him, he would work tirelessly toward the goal of earning that love. But asked to write a 10-year (even a 2-year) life plan, he looks to Ira, who always has the answer for everything. Where should they live? Upper east side. What color should the bath towels be? Black, to complement the clean chrome of the recently renovated bathroom hardware. Where will they go to dinner, and what should Eliot wear? Las Flores, with a bright green bowtie. The color makes his eyes pop and looks good next to Ira's tailored tweed. Good without being too matchy-matchy. Ira plans their vacations and says when Eliot's sister can visit (the only person to whom Eliot is out). Eliot does not feel deprived of power because he's willingly given it all to Ira—just one of the many gifts he's given his lover this year, to show his love. Just because Ira doesn't show his love in the same way, doesn't mean Ira doesn't love Eliot. And that is okay. Ira takes care of 'things' and Eliot takes care of Ira.

Last month, before a wedding reception for two of Ira's newly-nuptialed friends, Eliot had weakly protested his own appearance at the social event. "I won't know anyone there," he'd said. "You'll have more fun without me." Or that biggie: "You know I hate having my picture taken." Photos are proof that things happened, and were real. For that reason, Eliot loves being behind the camera, capturing in still moments the world as he sees it and sharing, in that way, his own reality with Ira, who takes at least a cursory interest in Eliot's art. But Eliot hates being the subject, the photographed. He doesn't care for how he looks in photos (always a little lost) or how they tie him to places and people both irrevocably and out of context: the frame never captures what was happening off-camera, which makes or breaks any story. Wedding receptions—especially gay ones—are notorious for flashy decor and noisy photographers who see too much: unspoken jealousies, secret affairs, drunken drama. Eliot had wanted no part of it, especially because Mr. and Mr. Blankenthal's wedding would (and did) make the society section.

"You ready?" Ira had yelled that night from the bedroom.

"Yes," Eliot had replied softly. He'd been ready for ten minutes, waiting patiently on the couch for Ira to finish primping.

"Help," Ira had said, walking into the room, tie extended. Ira could tie a tie, of course, but Eliot did it better and Eliot liked feeling useful.

"What'd you get them?" Ira had asked while Eliot worked.

"A Valentino bowl."

Ira had smiled, pleasantly surprised. "That's perfect. They'll love that."

Eliot had finished tucking Ira's tie into his vest, and Ira had kissed him. A rare moment of ebullience.

LORRIE doesn't worry about AIDS because it's 2016 and HIV long ago ceased being a hot-button topic. Sure, she knows its not 'just' gay men who get the disease—she saw *Dallas Buyers Club*[58]—but AIDS is so 1980s. Ebola and the Zika virus—hell, even Chipotle's continued E. coli outbreaks!—are ever so much more pressing. If a guy says he can't come wearing a condom, she doesn't force the issue. Skin-on-skin always feels better anyway. Aside from a tussle with the all-pervasive HPV, that scourge of the early 2000s infecting 75% of the sexually-active American population, and one case of molluscum[59] that while unsightly was not dangerous, she's been downright lucky. Oh, and only a couple pregnancy scares. Minor ones. A day or two of panic at most before her period arrived, the playful minx.

The problem is (and at 32, Lorrie is just beginning to realize this), she thinks every one is The One. If they show any promise at all in bed, if their breath doesn't make her shy away in horror, if they take semi-decent care of themselves, have a job—the basics!—that's all she asked for. She'd even been known to overlook one of the basics if it meant everlasting love. It never does though. Or hasn't at least. Not that she'll never find it. And there, that eternally hopeful romantic, positive in fallow periods that no one will ever want her again, sure when the new guy comes around that they'll live happily ever after. The back-and-forth, up-and-down threatens to tear her heart out every time. Only by her bootstraps does she recover: sheer stubborn will. Until the next time, when it starts all over again.

---

[58] A 2013 American biographical drama, the film tells the story of Ron Woodroof, an AIDS patient diagnosed in the mid-1980s when HIV/AIDS treatments were under-researched and the disease was highly stigmatized.

[59] Sometimes called water warts; a viral infection of the skin and occasionally of the mucous membranes.

Just to be sure, and because she's recently entered a new relationship, Lorrie's doctor recommends a blood test at her next Well Woman exam.

"A blood test? What for?"

"Oh, cholesterol, kidney and liver function, a general health panel."

"Oh."

"Also HIV."

"Oh?"

Lorrie's a fucking nervous wreck for the week it takes the office to call with the results. Ear pressed to the phone on a Friday, Lorrie sinks to the floor, pale and crying.

For seven long and utterly torturous days, much worse than any pregnancy scare (abortions are a thing even if a last resort; AIDS, on the other hand, is a death sentence), she convinces herself that God is punishing her for her indulgent, indiscriminate ways. She doesn't even believe in God, her mother did, but she can get behind a vengeful universe theory. For 7 days, Lorrie runs through her mind every single time she'd been sick with something remotely like the flu (it wasn't many), as she'd read that was the first symptom following HIV exposure. She'd had a cold just a month ago, but it'd been a legitimate cold, with congestion and drainage, not just a fever and body aches. If AIDS could be induced by thought/fear alone, Lorrie would contract it. When the not guilty verdict finally comes down, she collapses all right. Is even disbelieving. Most people, on hearing they've been infected, will ask, "But are you sure?!" Lorrie, on hearing that she had not, fairly screamed, "But how can you know?! What if you're wrong?!"

GEORGE hasn't eaten for 24 hours. He's abstained from alcohol, caffeine, sex, and electronics. George is ready for the shaman to work her magic.

300+ days out of the year, the shaman is a lawyer named **MONICA LIGHTFOOT**. She's 42, very pretty, with straight black hair that falls to her hips and hasn't a single strand of gray. Professionally-speaking, she's won 96% of her court cases, a near statistical improbability. Rumors circulate of Monica's using magic to sway her juries, but of course it's never been proven. Modern-day courtrooms protect their borders with metal detectors and concern themselves with keeping out weapons and keeping in the system the accused. No one asks Ms. Lightfoot about the tiny leather pouch at her neck, the mementos—the magic—she keeps inside it.

Approximately sixty days out of the year, Monica exchanges her tailored suit for a rag dress. Her long hair, normally secured in a tight plaited bun, blows wild as the wind on an empty plains night, tangling with her crown of dove white feathers, clicking with the weight of threaded blood clay beads. She is not Ms. Lightfoot on these occasions, but Nihimá, our Mother. A terrible, world-ending karmic mother, blue eyes blazing and fire in her fingertips. At such times as George dares to look at her, Monica appears nothing like her sweet-though-strong civilian self. She is a woman possessed—a conduit for some power far greater than George or Monica, and hopefully great enough to contend with whatever malevolent force seems intent on sucking the joy from George's twilight years. Such joy as he can have, anyway, without Sarah.

The language that Nihimá chants is not recognizable as English or Navajo. It's more guttural than that, stabbing into the black sky and wrapping George in a straightjacket of irrational fear. He wants Monica's (Nihimá's) intervention. He trusts her. But he's heard what can happen when one aggravates intentionally a sleeping monster.

Nihimá directs him to lie on a woven mat near the fire. They are outside, but George can barely make out the stars this close to the light. As he tries to relax, his old body creaks and groans settling into and against the contours of the ground. One particularly sharp rock juts just under his right shoulder blade, but watching Nihimá from the corner of his eye, George doesn't dare move.

The instant the shaman cups her hands over George's ears, the ringing stops. For what feels like at least five glorious minutes, he knows nothing but beautiful, merciful silence. The silence that must have existed before sound. Pre-dawn, Bible-black silence. It's like being dead and buried and back in the womb all at once. A bliss he never wants to leave, and the desire to start living anew—to reclaim the life he'd lost to old age and the cruel tricks of coyote-hearted spirits.

She packs something cool and damp into his ears. Soothes the auricle folds like the folds of mitochondrial DNA. Great Mother, going home.

When her two favorite masked lovers enter **LORRIE**'s room, Larry the frog burps a cherry hello. That's why Lorrie will later believe it had to be real: their nocturnal visit, emerging bent double from a tiny door in the wall, **HANNAH**'s full breasts rounding above a black leather bustier, the tiny door in the wall definitely not there the next morning. Lorrie has just time enough to reflect that only terrifying things come through tiny doors: trolls and little doll-shaped monsters and, *shudder*, human children.

There's a knock from what would normally be the bathroom, just on the other side of the wall. Then the door opens and out crawl those two beautiful creatures, nothing monster-like about them at all.

Except for their appetites. Those appear insatiable. And the only food they seem to need is Lorrie.

This time it's her legs they bind in hospital-grade cuffs, tightening the belt cinches until no blood can possibly squeeze through. Her feet so unfeelingly thick after awhile that they might as well not be there. As they then fasten her restraints around the posterior bed posts, Lorrie thinks briefly of Paul Sheldon[60] in *Misery*, his ankles bound to a block then snapped with the dull end of a sledgehammer. She sees again the guillotine that wavers above her like a promise. At the peak of her orgasm, two tongues and twenty fingers attending to her most sensitive parts, the blade falls with a most satisfying speed.

---

[60] The protagonist of Stephen King's *Misery*; a writer famous for Victorian-era romance novels involving the character of Misery Chastain.

"Herein do we bathe in sleep, sinking back into the primordial deep, returning to forgotten things before time was: and the soul is renewed, touching the Great Mother. Whoso cannot return to the primordial, hath no roots in life, but withereth as the grass. These are the living dead, they who are orphaned of the Great Mother."
—DION FORTUNE, *ASPECTS OF OCCULTISM*

On Friday, **CAPTAIN HOOK** hosts a Dallas pop-up, the details again disseminated last minute via a buried website. He has no new gadgets to debut this time, but his lab partner, inspired by their Southern Americana surroundings, has come up with the theme of Texas Chainsaw. Bartholomew wears a baggy mask pieced together from the tanned hides of last week's limb donors.

In the 1960s, Austin's Texas State Hospital saw fit to begin harvesting the brains of its mental patients for "research purposes" upon their deaths. Each brain was plunked in a jar of formaldehyde, labeled with a number that corresponded to the patient's file, and occasionally a description of whatever medical anomaly afflicted that patient. From microcephaly to Alzheimers, meningitis to the prefrontal lobotomy, doctors could theoretically learn how to better treat the living. The jars were sealed with glue, stored in a cool, dark place, and forgotten about.

Until one day almost thirty years later, a newly-hired janitor went looking for the extra cleaning supplies and opened the closet that no one had in all that time. Imagine the dead smell of old chemicals and older parts, dust thick as wrapping paper that begged removal before one could see properly inside.

Who knows with whom the janitor shared his unusual find? Slowly the jars started walking off: there is a market for human organs. A whole lot of money could have been gleaned from the sale of Charles Whitman's brain.[61] The "Tower Shooter," he shot and killed 17 people from the tower on the University of Texas campus in 1966. His brain has yet to be recovered.

[61] During the autopsy, Dr. Chenar discovered a brain tumor (approx. the size of a pecan) that may have affected Whitman's homicidal actions.

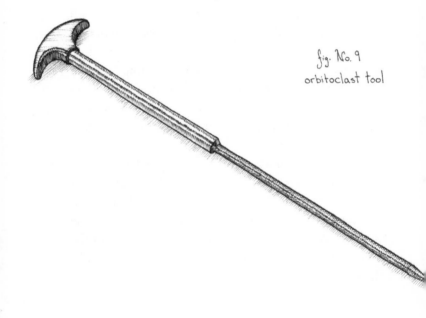

fig. No. 9
orbitoclast tool

In 2014, grand theft human also hit the Indiana Medical History Museum in Indianapolis. The thief put the preserved organs for sale on eBay. Four brains went to an enthusiast in California. When the jars arrived, he noted with suspicion the call numbers on their bases. He tracked them back to the museum in Indiana, and then supplied what information he had about the seller to local authorities, who eventually detained David Charles[62] and his stolen goods.

[62] A California man arrested after allegedly stealing human brain samples from a history museum and selling them on eBay.

Before her hand replacement surgery, **ANNA** dreamed of an eBay for limbs. If she could only visit the sterile white store of the internet, scroll through color-coded pages of viable wrists, palms, and fingers, cobbling together a custom order the way one might do with a pair of Nike shoes, then bidding according to means, or how great your need was—how badly you wanted a part. In 2010, they would've all been salvaged, donated limbs. By 2016, they're growing single limbs from stem cells that no one had to die to donate. Giving birth to the designer limb, and eventually, the elective plastic surgery. Then one day, the designer body.

Sometimes there's a phantom limb and sometimes there's a cure for a phantom limb. Somewhere a man searches through a pile of severed legs, collected and stacked and called "Heyday." He thinks, If I can find mine, I might finally scratch the itch, ever growing, forever maddening.

Once a man with a phantom arm, believing the limb to be paralyzed and invisible, realized that if he reflected his good arm in a mirror placed just so, it would appear as though his missing hand could open, grasp, and clasp. It was a mind trick and proved conclusively the power of illusion over the psyche, over the core beliefs that make us who we are.

Amusingly (horrifyingly?) the man who felt his phantom limb finally disappear was left with tiny fingers growing psychically from a shoulder stump. Little fingerlets. Fingerlings? Fingerings?

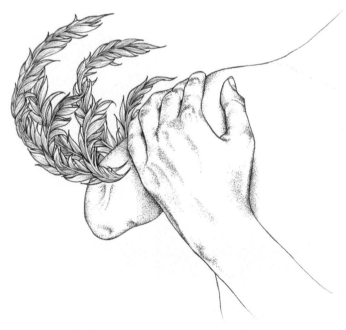

IRA has a name now for when **ELIOT** (eventually) expertly cuts off blood flow to his cock. He calls it fingering, a term which brings him no small ironic pleasure.

On Friday, **GEORGE** slips beneath the shaman's spell like a tightly woven and beautifully dyed Navajo blanket.

He's walking down a train track. Squatting to let the cool wave of water lap at his bare balls. He prepares for six years' hard labor in a Soviet camp turning big rocks into itty bitty rocks.

With each step, grapes crush under his feet, spilled onto headstones.

Over there: a pile of antlers.

George, he's a stuffed donkey watching a boy climb a ladder with a book. Painting chickens red while their feathers are still attached.

Oil drips from his Roman beard like diamonds. Mandolins spin in thin air.

We are searching for ourselves in each other. Lighting white paper roses on fire.

He wishes to suck from the shell teat of the nun in white lace.

And I—I came for your ghost stories. What makes a place the #1 most-haunted in New York City? Number of recorded experiences? Are those experiences pre- or post-exposure to the power of suggestion? Do you have a snotty green trickster named Slimer? Is he a skinwalker?

Stark naked, his skin red and cracked as the earth he lies on, George opens his mouth to scream. Whether any sound dribbles forth is uncertain. George cannot hear himself over the ringing, and there is no one else to hear the screaming, not out here in the middle of nowhere. No one else to smell the sick BBQ smell of George's back skin fusing with rock so hot you could "fry an egg on it," and hotter still. When he rolls into a fetal position sometime later, his body leaves a layer, like a solar shadow or the egg skin crusted to the frying pan that wasn't well-oiled before use.

The shaman's skin is pale as ice now, George sees—and her eyes. Those cannot be **MONICA**'s eyes. He will marry her anyway, on the front lawn, as children play pie-pan tambourines and crow women have their necks waxed.

In the land of the dead, horses buck like unicorns. Soot swarms like (bug) plague from the bodies of corpses.

In a waxbuilt castle of love, in the monastery, brothers eat pomegranates like pussy.

A very live mule grinds corn and baptizes silent babes in quicksilver.

Grief, grief, grief.

George, he's keeping the snakes from biting each other. All the men who look like corpses finally expire.

A poured gold hand, the ring finger missing. A camel with two humps scarlet, drips the blood.

Oh, hai, doggy!

An old man descends the ladder

and yet again a boy.

For a skull with hair, you're okay.

"Merry," in American, means "die."

On Thursday, **ELIOT** goes to work at the courthouse. He wears the tailored navy blazer and the Italian leather shoes that Ira had picked out to match the soft leather belt—a first Christmas present. Cinching it around his thin waist that morning, Eliot had thought about what it meant to cut something off, whether a train of thought or an act of speech. Split ends or a price tag. Or blood flow to a cock.

Sometimes cutting is utilitarian and sometimes it's an act of violence. Sometimes as natural as cutting a fat rind from a pork chop. Sometimes as wholly unnatural as watching the parts of someone you love be manipulated, tortured, made bruised and engorged and purple with the effort of a body to keep on living, to function as it has since the closing of the circulatory system en utero.

He had asked himself how cutting off was different from cutting out. The excision of a cancerous mass from healthy tissue, or of a friend from a well-established peer group. One could also cut in, he had surmised, to a line of people or a line of coke. Into the arteries that rail-road up the wrists. Every day of his life is an exercise in cutting through: office bullshit, backed-up traffic, the crippling anxiety not of being single and gay, but of loving a man with whom he feels more alone than when single.

Worst of all, everything, someday, will end up on the cutting room floor. He knows that in the final accounting of Ira's life, when he is an old man, distinguished and yet beautiful, there will be no room for Eliot, the extraneous footage.

The next time **LORRIE** sees **CAPTAIN HOOK** perform, she realizes two things: one, she likes (really likes) sleeping with the son of a bitch; and two—he's stolen her material!

"The guy with the prosthetic leg pretends to want to shake my hand but trips me instead. I am strangled by his neckties."
—KIM YIDEUM

Close your eyes. Fall asleep.

Have a dream that feels so real your pussy aches for perfect dream dick.

Have a dream that cannot be real except to say, "You are everything I ever wanted plus Kim's dead cat." See through closed eyelids the tools spread like a fairy feast in Pan's underground labyrinth. Beware the Moorchild who appeals to your sense of aesthetics.

"The scalpel," she says, with blonde eyes. "The scalpel is clean. It's about control."

While she's right, check out the hacksaw before you make a decision. Heft it. Feel the well-balanced weight and upwelling of teeth like an unzipped mouth stretched and grinning. Consider what it means to bite into. Rip away in stringy jerky-strips the seams of yourself that have too long walked in the light.

Pull a Sally. Pull the string that binds elbow to forearm. What will the surgeon demand? Sterile, or quick?

Barring the morphine of a better year, the alien technology of nano-drills and pinched skin, blood flow like a quickening, a pinning betraying. An intact capillary system, a closed circulatory system—a body whole.

Or choose the gun.

The hammer and chisel.

The iron so red-hot it cauterizes as it cuts.

Pick the butcher knife. Place on block offending knuckle. Toe. Tongue.

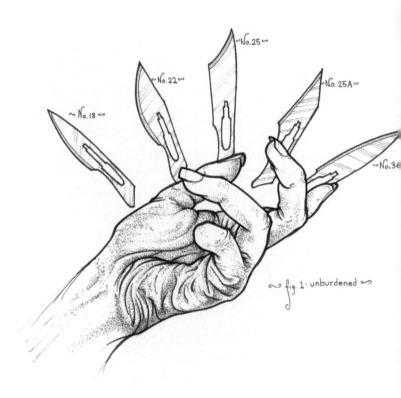

~No.25~

~No.22~

~No.18~

~No.25A~

~No.36~

~fig. 1: unburdened~

Play a hand of pinochle with dibs on the jar of pig knuckles and as the warm-up noise of a pre-show symphony begins its mid-stage cacophony, lift and wave your bloody stump like "Anything you can do, I can do better; I can do anything better than you."

Stand *en pointe*. Into ballerina shoes with wooden forms insert one hairy, toe-free foot and shout, "Eureka! This is how you dance!" Spin and twirl and kick a veined leg high, flinging droplets as you do, wood block and pink satin now positively saturated (game show host) as a leech that drank too much and then exploded. Greed is a sin for a reason.

Gluttony and lust are sins for a reason, called vice because they are nice, doing a body good, doing the whole world the favor of being, at long last, you. Imperfect until made perfect. Shaped. Whittled. Carved like a Thanksgiving turkey. Will you choose the electric meat knife, blade brr-ing?

Every tool has a purpose. Purpose denoting intelligent design. Consciousness sparked long after conception, in the eating of an apple, at the encouragement of a snake.

Kiss her who made it so you know, now, everything. Not your nakedness, which is holy, but that which preempts your happily ever after: your wholly ever after.

Look up, and out, and down from the bridge. Straight into the eyes of your executioners—what gleam you can see through the slit of black hood over neutral face but determined posture. The gloved hand of the gallows man. The cleats and footy jersey of talent reborn as terror, redeemed in the blood of the lamb.hand.man.

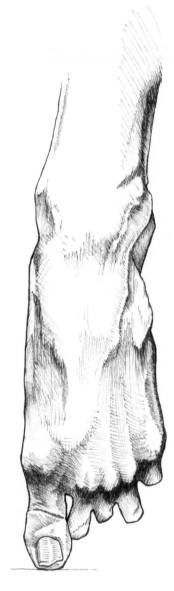

fig No. 13 ~ En Pointe

When doctors palpate
When larvae pupate
They're feeling for
Seeking out
The same thing:
Someone to come home to.

Not another being. Another body. The identity that fits like the gallows man's glove. Feeling not so tumor-ish as the neat edge of an ending. A landing on which to step out and greet the night.

A person dies when her brain dies. Everything else is replaceable.

You'd think that two women with the same low-stress profession (Franciscan nun), same exercise habits (walking meditation), same diet (bland, and built around bran) would maintain roughly the same figure. But **SR. M**. has swollen ankles, pale even beneath her hose and stuffed into well-worn Teva sandals. Next to her, **SR. J**. looks almost birdlike, all tiny grace and a tinier tattoo on her ribs that for all their modesty none of the other sisters know about. So, hormones—even in women who aren't having sex—must be a real and defining thing. Sr. M. looking like (because she is biological sister to) Big Tub of the folds and slabs of flesh. Sr. J. having no known relations to which to compare herself (she was adopted) may or may not be underweight for her frame. May or may not have been inspired by that 1992 made-for-TV movie about the bulimic girl who stores her vomit in jars in her closet (what, asking to be caught?). It's not that Sr. J. has an eating disorder; it's that eating makes her sick to her stomach—how nauseating to introduce to God's vessel dirty green veg plucked from the ground or dripping red meat (also ground). These may be from the same dust as that from which Christ had sculpted Sr. J., but they are not of the purified dust, the ashes to which Sr. J. is steadily returning her nose in particular and more quickly than the rest, shredded by too-often coke consumption. The drug helps the endless rosaries fly by, helps dull the prick of **FR. W**.'s sermons (literally perfect in their ratio of guilt-to-wet-dream-inducing delivery), poking at her virginal nether regions like Satan the snake himself. It is the intermittent nosebleeds that prompt her sisters to express their concern: does Sr. J. feel okay? Is she having headaches? "Just allergies," she waves them off, smiling, teeth closed so as not to betray the way her tongue is turning black at the back, acid-eaten and burnt from cocaine chemtrails dripping down her throat like cum she's never tasted.

Ironically, it was the woman she'd been trying to save who had in fact saved Sr. J.. "How do you know cocaine is bad unless you try it?" **JUNG-IL** had asked. Just a bump, feeling like Adam accepting just a bite. When Jung-il had laughed, her surgically-split tongue had poked from her lip-ring studded mouth with an invitation: "Won't you have a taste of knowledge, little lamb? Just a lick. A line. Look how white, how pure, how good."

Lollipops. Hard candy. Lemons.

It's not about deciding but allowing a thing to be true in the moment.

The wheels of the chakra extend fingers to my eyelids and other extremities.

Fear, like lemons, is yellow. Yellow-belly quivering aspen—the baby's eyes flutter then relax.

Take St. John's Wort[63] for nightmares. Perhaps the nightmare is the life we're living.

Yellow is the color of a car slowing down at a traffic stop. The deceleration and the slight jerk forward. Maybe even the hesitation of deciding whether or not to floor it at the last second. Yellow is the color of wanting a woman you love very much to say 'yes' when you pop that question. Yellow is the color of a dog rolling over, belly-up, for a stomach scratch or in surrender to a stronger animal. Yellow is the color of your tongue going prickly after a squeeze of lemon, or the bitter bite of vinegar and other acids. Yellow is the color of taffeta on a prom dress in the '80s. Smell the hairspray and the make-up caked on so thick you'd have to cut it if it were custard for dessert. Yellow is the color of hot sand on a salty beach, and the satin, peeling wallpaper that kept Charlotte a prisoner before they knew what postpartum depression was. Strong nerves and a spinal cord.

---

[63] A medicinal herb with antidepressant activity and potent anti-inflammatory properties.

It's good luck to sit in vomit on a first date.

She doesn't say anything. She's mute. Are the stories running out? Is there nothing new left to say? Is she smiling, but, sadly, emptyheaded? Am I emptyheaded? I chose wallpaper. It's more interesting. A color and a texture. Floral—isn't all wallpaper? Get the word out. The non-word. Oh my. She's me. Nothing left to say. Is silence bliss? Protest? Accept.

There was the Indian guy who told me all about cobras in baskets but I don't remember the details. Families over there maybe still practice trades and you're born into the family business and one of them is snake-handling. They might sit in a pit of hissing vipers and either build up their immunity by drinking a little venom extract every day or playing as children around the hornet's nest, which is just a different but equally painful prick. The snakes are gods so they won't bite the hands that feed them or the bodies that lay prostrate on bellies even smoother than snakeskin.

Our skin protects us from nothing. Porous, bacteria slip through with ease. Bellies so unresistingly punctured by knife, sword—the Indian equivalent of seppuku.

On the mountain there was an ashram.

In the ashram there was a guru.

The guru knelt before a statue draped in garlands and swimming in sugar cubes.

Fangs unlike incisors are not as good for tearing. Only puncturing. Immobilizing. Swallowing whole through the distended jaws of some deep-sea eel. Are snakes prehistoric? What does it mean to have lived before history, and to still live today? What are you proof of apart from the fact that sandalwood still smells like sandalwood even after all this time? Centuries flew, then centuries of men who walked upright only to crawl on their bellies and devolve back into tweeting, sniveling things. I am a reptile. I need heat like oxygen, to warm blood that only boils infrequently—though always on bad dates.

Do you feel the snake slipping through your fingers? A long rope of sleek muscle, more multidirectional than a penis in heat (which knows only in-out, poke-retreat, hungry but scared and so it steals its sustenance in tipsy, greedy gulps.)

What of the basket? Handwoven by another family whose trade has always been basketweaving and maybe they make a better living because while they're not pimping gods, everyone needs a basket, and as with any skill there are novices and masters, and our Indian basket weavers, they're masters. All the way. They howl in high-pitched synchronicity with the inserting of one straw through one band.

A whole family makes a basket, from the harvest and drying and dyeing of straw, to the framing and weaving and lid-fitting with bells so a family of cobras curls up in one basket, sharing or stealing each other's heat (since in nature, every creature lives for itself—humankind, by the way, only pretends to have evolved past truth to al-truism). Yes, taste that word. Stinky as kava. Then choke on its overly mineralized content (please).

E. shot a snake and skinned it, peeling the scale-sock off in one reverse full-sleeve then rolling it back up Pita's arm like an arm-warmer, except it was the tropics, except it was Arizona, except India is both tropical and a desert and that's why the baskets are so many colors: reflecting flower pistil-stamen rub-a-dubbing in a co-lonial metal tub. Puja bells are hand-poured and forged and how many hands do you suppose were lost to the pouring and forging? How many snake skins? How many rattles amputated from tails, docked like dogs' waggers, docked like Miewes the German cannibal cut Brandes's tallywhacker?

What did it smell like, frying in oil and flour? What

did the rattle sound like, shaking yet with the electrical impulses of newly-severed muscle, nerves firing reflexively?

When the cobra rears, A. stares, hypnotized.

When the cobra strikes, he jumps reflexively.

But a clumsy human can never outmaneuver a striking snake.

That's biology.

That's the food chain.

One big joke.

Cobra venom mainlined like heroin without the orgasm. If only it made a 3-inch section of flesh around the bite mark rot and fall off. Then Big Tub could go to India to have his pounds literally melted away. Or, because he might not (definitely won't) fit in an airplane seat, India can come to him. In NYC. In San Francisco. All those Silicon Valley brownies secretly (longingly) stroking their cobras at night, scratching beneath their hoods, muttering sweet nothings into the oblivion of a California night.

Tyler Durden made soap but I want to make art, smearing your monthly (the bloodletting of an amputated egg).

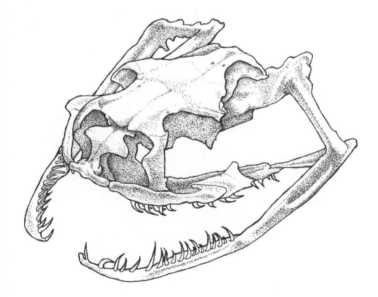

Photographs capture souls, not smiles.

Local attempts at exorcism weren't working. By the time the Vatican gets involved, **SR. J.** is pronounced corporeally dead. Maybe her soul is still in her body. Maybe the Devil has claimed it for himself. Either way, to make sure that her corpse is not supernaturally reanimated, they have to cut off her head.

Jenny[64] wore a green ribbon around her neck. The nun wears a strand of rosary beads. When Alfred removed the green ribbon, Jenny's head fell off. When **FR. W.** removes the strand of blessed beads, Sr. J.'s face immediately loses the bloom of good health. In case the rosary was somehow protecting her (or him from her), he braids the beads into her hair. Sr. J.'s hair is mostly gray with hints of blonde yet, and is surprisingly long. Fr. W. had never seen Sr. J.'s hair before, hidden as it always had been beneath the black veil of her habit. He pauses to caress her familiar face tenderly, and to reflect on how very well you could know someone without really knowing the person at all. When the braiding is complete, he places the heavy stone crucifix at the tail end of the rosary on Sr. J.'s forehead. Fr. W. leaves to let the surgeon do his work.

DR. C. palms the super fine scalpel. Its edge so sharp that at only a couple microns thick, it exceeds the visible spectrum. Using such a tool will allow the good doctor to sever the microscopic fibers of the spinal cord cleanly. It would not do to butcher.mutilate.desecrate the body of a holy woman.

As Dr. C. makes the first cut, he sends a whispered prayer for protection to HEAVEN. Not to God in Heaven, but to Dr. Canavero, inventor of the HEad Anastomosis VENture. Anastomosis is the surgical connecting of two parts. A hand to a wrist, for example. A head to a body.

---

[63] from: Alvin Schwartz, *In a Dark, Dark Room and Other Scary Stories.*

Dr. C.'s orders are to mummify Sr. J.'s severed head. So preserved, it may be 'watched over' by the Catholic Church for signs of unholy activity, while the rest of her body is properly buried. Dr. C., however, has different plans.

He wants to know what it's like to be possessed. With such knowledge, he figures, one might turn the tables. Might in turn possess the powers of the possessor. Of the thing that tortured poor Sr. J. in life.

If he can only reattach her head to a new body, a non-possessed donor body, keeping "Sr. J." alive long enough to hear her speak, the secrets of heaven and hell and of the whole fucking universe could be his.

"It's not like you can unscrew your head and put it on someone else." The condescending voice and words of Arthur Caplan, Ph.D., director of medical ethics at NYU's Langone Medical Center, haunt.taunt.distract the back of his mind. "I would not allow anyone to do it to me as there are a lot of things worse than death."

Beef jerky, wrapped in silk and rewoven rosary beads.

"It might seem obvious, but in order to carry out the transplant you need to sever the spinal cord, which renders people paralyzed from the neck down. If a person isn't already paralyzed that's an incredibly risky thing to do."

Dr. C. wheels the stiff, draped in a demure white sheet, up to the operating room. No one stops him to ask about the body because not even doctors or nurses like death. Moreover, it is widely conceded that Dr. C takes each death under his watch or on his table quite personally, blaming himself for the inevitable outcome of an impossible situation. If he is seen wheeling a draped gurney through the halls, likely his patient has just died and so it is best not to approach the surgeon for anything. Especially not to ask some ignorant question like, 'Say, who's the cold one, Doc?' Dr. C. therefore makes his transfer uninterrupted, and brings the body of John Doe, 58, DOA, drunk-driving victim (he'd been the drunk) to rest beside that of J. Dalloway, 66, formerly possessed.

The surgery takes 34 hours. Dr. C. never once pauses in his work. He's given himself a urine catheter, colostomy bag, and IV drip just for the purpose of being able, for as long as necessary, to forgo the limitations and urgent calls to action of the human body. Sleep is unthinkable given the overdose levels of adrenaline coursing through his body. By 7:30 PM, he is drenched in sweat and starting to smell, as are the two bodies in their stainless steel cradles. Kept cryogenically frozen for the past several weeks, they are thawing now like Thanksgiving turkeys, skin puckered and damp and squishier with every hour. It's why Dr. C. beheads John Doe first—it isn't so important for his dismemberment to be as smooth. A couple jagged artery-threads or uneven mastoid muscle flaps here and there don't matter, as they'll be sewn up and around Sr. J.'s corresponding parts. Her cuts require a much smoother precision, so he attends to her second—once her warming flesh gives more readily to the scalpel's seductive love bite. When she doesn't resist in the least, Dr. C. smiles and pats her head.

Good girl, Joan.

Reattachment is the most time-consuming procedure. He places each head on a wheeled cart, then swaps them. (If you were wondering, a human head weighs 11 pounds on average.) He leaves Sr. J.'s body and John Doe's head to sit in their respective juices while he begins the delicate task of transplantation. It doesn't have to be perfect; Dr. C. will not require his monster to live for long. But the sutures have to be tight enough to keep most of their re-combined blood and guts in the proper channels. A second death by sepsis, so soon after resurrection, would not do.

Dr. C. connects the carotid to the carotid, the jugular to the jugular. Uses lasers to fuse—in painstaking
detail—the fibers of the spinal cord. Glues trapezius to
scalene. And finally, delirious from fatigue, rather messily
closes the 360-degree ring around their necks and throats,
tying off the bright green thread with a sigh that betrays
no small exhaustion. He peels off his sticky latex gloves,
turns on the warmer panel beneath the horror (it is hard
even for him to look at that soft gray-blonde hair piled
gracefully around the burly, hairy tattooed shoulders of a
man whom no one will miss). He lays down on the OR
floor, pulls the morgue drape over himself for comfort,
and rests his eyes for no more than 15 minutes.

Four hours later, the delicious smell of roasting meat
lures Dr. C. back awake. Despite the nutrient-rich IV drip,
his stomach growls hungrily, and he props himself up on
one arm, feeling his back groan and his eyes blink rapidly.

Everything comes back to him in a rush. Dr. C. jumps
up, getting tangled in and tripping over his shroud in the
process, and runs to the steel bay. Right away he can see
that the warmer panel has been on too high and for too
long. The back, sides, shoulders, and feet of John Doe
have blistered, taking on the cracked-but-caramelized appearance of a perfectly-done but still moist bird. Most of
Sr. J.'s hair has curled up, blackened and burnt away. The
back of her skull is visible where the high heat has eaten
through her thin scalp-skin. All of this Dr. C. takes in
peripherally while gaping at the goriest aspect yet: Sr. J.'s
eyes. They're open.

Quickly, Dr. C. ascertains what must have happened.
Heat causes things (especially damp things) to expand. As
Sr. J.'s eye jelly had cooked, her ocular membranes had
bulged with the expansion of liquid to gas, causing them
to pop out through the lids he'd failed to superglue shut.

A very dead shade of yellow, her pupils see nothing. Yet.

Praying it is not too late, Dr. C rips the automatic defibrillator from the wall. He places the sticky cups of the heart rate monitor on John Doe's flabby chest. He flips the switch on the ADF, holds the paddles at the ready, then delivers 500 volts of electricity straight to John Doe's heart. The body jumps on the table like a gasping fish, or a dog flopping belly-up for a rub.

Nothing else happens. The body again resumes the texture and consistency of an oven-fresh pork loin.

Dr. C tries again. 800 volts.

The body leaps almost a foot off the table.

A heartbeat registers on the monitor.

Dr. C. literally watches the blood start to flow again through John Doe's curdled veins. The tiny blue rivulets beneath the skin of his inner elbows momentarily bulge then flatten again. He times the seconds it will take for the blood flow to complete one circuit, noting with satisfaction that no blood leaks from the good sister's neck. He'd done a good job on the circulatory system. If the body suffers from any internal bleeding, it is due to injuries sustained during the car accident—not from incompetence on Dr. C.'s part. He remembers to turn the warming panel off and the ventilator on. John Doe's chest rises and falls rhythmically. Sr. J.'s cheeks puff out ever so slightly with each intubated inhalation. He transfers his own catheter and IV drip to the monster. As the body gradually cools to a healthier 98 degrees, the nun's eye jelly condenses and her lids softly close. If not for the neat ring of stitches around the conjoined neck, or the fact that the head of a plainly pretty woman now sits atop the torso of public enemy #1, Dr. C. would have said that everything is right with the world, so peaceful does his little monster look.

And tasty.

Unable to fight the compulsion any longer, Dr. C. leaves for a burger at the 24-hour hospital cafeteria. It's been a day and then some.

He returns 45 minutes later to find the formerly inviting smell of cooked meat replaced by the now more pervasive smell of John Doe's rotting head and Sr. J.'s putrefying body cavity. He quickly wraps these in the crumpled morgue sheet and drags them to the incinerator hatch at the end of the hallway.

While he is gone, Sr. J. opens her bloodshot eyes. She yawns, uncoiling a forked black tongue. She stretches John Doe's arms above her head and in front of his body in the air. She sits up and shakes what's left of her long gray-blonde hair, uncovered during the daylight hours for the first time in 48 years. Blood mats the locks in places, but no worries—her Father will understand. When she stands, she realizes that John Doe is naked, and it is good. Everything the doctor has created is good. She feels no shame, but testing her balance, sets out to explore the hospital garden.

NATANJALI brings the blade to her chest unhesitatingly. "I'll do it," she says, pressing knife edge to flesh mound.

"No, daughter," her father consoles her. "We will find the money. I could not let you destroy any precious thing, least of all the most precious thing."

Natanjali looks at him with questions in her eyes and in her heart.

"You, pita." V. shakes his head sadly. "Blood of my blood."

He starts walking away, muttering in the old tongue: "So, so beautiful. So, so wrong."

Natanjali lays the knife down with a sigh. Its carved bone handle, inlaid with emeralds, winks in the morning light. Another day, another dollar. Another din, another rupee. But they'll never get the monkey that is Britain off India's back. She'd bowed too easily under the weight of aristocracy. Natanjali fears that India could no longer straighten her shoulders if she tried. So she straightens her own shoulders, and goes to soothe the crying babe in the next room.

As she passes through the kitchen, Natanjali nods at her cousin. P. squats on the floor above a different blade, this one mounted to a wooden block. She is using it to painstakingly dice garlic, one clove at a time. The spicy smell is so strong that Natanjali's eyes water, disguising any lingering angry tears. Twenty years Natanjali's senior, cousin P.'s breasts have lost any firmness they might once have had. Her teats hang like drained and long-empty dugs, like the milking goat's in the backyard after her fifth litter. Cartilage sucked down to a skin cask. While P. has nothing of which to be ashamed (her eldest son is now a doctor in America, where outdated structures like the caste system have no place), still Natanjali thinks that if a woman wants to cover her breasts like she covers her hair—a sign of respect to Shiva—then she ought to be able to dress in a way that also commands respect: that keeps her body holy and (wholly) hers. To be shared only with her husband. With their unweaned son. Rather than a display to be leered at, he had always made her feel like a work of art. A priceless creation to be pored over, appreciated, and worshipped in ecstatic detail. She wants to belong to her king; not to the king.

"Mohabbat," Natanjali says to P. "Throw me that rag."

P. pinches the corner of the kitchen towel that covers her lap. Natanjali pulls two pins from her hair and secures the towel so that it covers her breasts. Immediately she feels better. P. gives her a strange look but says nothing.

After attending to her son, Natanjali starts her morning chores. She sweeps the packed earth floors of their home. Picks mung beans from the garden to grind. Rinses the rice. Milks the buffalo. By late morning, the sun is high and hot. She pauses in her work to unpin the towel and pat dry her damp forehead with it. Thus occupied, she doesn't see the man in the suit approach on foot. He has a clipboard, leather shoes, and a monogrammed satchel. It is embroidered with the crest of the king.

"Natanjali Kripala Puerh?" he addresses her.

"Haan."

"You are hereby fined for flagrant impostership of a higher caste. The debt is due upon receipt."

He hands her a stamped sheet of yellow paper.

"Very well," he continues. "That counts as receipt. Please produce the amount indicated at once."

"But I'm not posing as anyone," Natanjali protests. "I answered to my name and that's who I am."

"Will you not pay?"

"No, I will not."

"Is your husband home?"

Natanjali's face flames. "He's not available at the moment, and I've done nothing wrong. Please leave now."

V. appears in the doorway. "Betee. Is everything okay?"

Fluent in the king's speech but not in the old tongue, the tax collector cannot understand their exchange. But he speaks body language, and notes how the old man's hackles have risen protectively.

"Mr. Puerh? Your daughter is in violation of the Breast Tax. Someone owes me money immediately."

V. looks at the royal decree in Natanjali's trembling hands.

"It is a towel, sir," he reasons. "A kitchen rag. She is only using it to pat her brow and shoo the flies away."

"No," the tax collector counters. "I have watched her all morning, daring to pretend that she is something she is not. The woman has broken the law, and disobedience now will result in only more severe repercussions." Everyone is silent for a moment while Natanjali glares at the ground, angered and ashamed despite her best efforts to remain above shame.

"We cannot pay," Vihaan says quietly.

"Then she will be jailed," the tax collector replies, and he grabs Natanjali's arm roughly to haul her to her feet.

"No!" V. yells, at the same moment that Natanjali's son begins to cry again from inside the hut.

"Please, mahoday," Natanjali says. "My son."

When the man in the suit only pulls her along anyway, V. steps in front of him. "Take me instead."

The tax collector considers. "Okay, but the fine will double. Two pounds."

Natanjali stares hard at the ground, willing herself not to cry or shout or tackle the tax man as he drags her pita away.

"I'll come for you," she finally says, though whether it is a promise to V. or a threat of revenge, not even Natanjali knows.

That night, after her boy and cousin P. are asleep, Natanjali goes to visit her husband's grave. She places three burning sticks of incense in a tiny wooden Ganesh head and sends it floating out onto the Ganges River. She thanks both God and her dead husband for everything they have given her—most especially her son.

"Two pounds," she announces, sliding a leather-bound bundle across the desk. It leaves a red smear.

"Now let my father go."

With a pencil, the warden flips back the bundle's flap.

"What the—?!" he covers his mouth and gags.

The tax collector watches this exchange from across the room. It is then that he notices Natanjali's still-covered chest. The sheer gall of the woman!

He strides swiftly across the room and with a yank tears the thick cloth binding the holes where Natanjali's breasts had been.

The tax collector steps back in horror.

"Try taxing me now," she says, before pushing past the ugly man in the empty suit.

LORRIE is at the mall when she sees her: an adult Filipino woman easily mistakable for a child. Her naturally small frame (had she still had legs) would have stood no more than five feet tall. But she doesn't have legs. Or arms. They've been 'taken,' all the way to hip and shoulder. No stumps. She is a torso in a wheelchair.

From her head to the toes she doesn't have, the woman maybe measures 30-odd inches. The average newborn measures 20-odd inches.

The woman probably knows that, though. It appears she's had four of her own children.

All skinny-limbed (and completely intact—as Mommy once must have been), the kids take turns pushing and walking alongside their mother's wheelchair. The straight black hair on their mini-me scalps swish in tandem with Mommy's, bumping softly over the pitted asphalt.

For the first time in her life, Lorrie experiences envy.

Forget the kind of role-playing that simulates helplessness. Lorrie might be bound five ways to Sunday until she loses sensation in her arms and legs both, but the next morning the limbs are still there. She's never been truly dependent on another human being since first being weaned from the breast.

This Filipino momma on the other hand—she can't do a thing for herself. Not cook, not eat, not wipe her ass, nor bathe. *Not hug her children goodnight, either,* Lorrie thinks a little sadly. But she could lay there. Be a warm and comforting presence, singing lullabies and kissing their foreheads. Her husband then could carry her out of the room like the babes he'd once laid in their cribs. *She's never done that,* Lorrie marvels. *Carried her babies to bed after carrying them in her womb.* She's never had to. Physically, he controls everything. His wife still has a voice, of course—

but does she use it? And does he hear it?

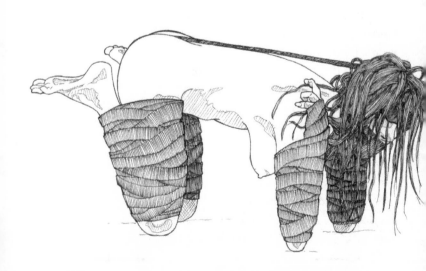

She's a sex toy. And a mother. But to become a mother she first had to become a sex toy. And to become a sex toy she first had to become a quadruple amputee: little more than some holes and a sac of organs. A beautiful mind in a mutilated body.

Elective amputation. Lorrie feels sure of it.

She realizes that Mommy is staring back at her. Not with hostility and not with warmth, but neutrally. *This is how I present myself to the world*, she seems to be saying. She doesn't need Lorrie's—or anyone's—external validation. She has her love, and the products of that love: four attractive, healthy, and well-behaved kids.

On Wednesday, Lorrie posts a poll to a fetish site: "If you could be a nugget, would you?" There's a text box in which to elaborate why/why not.

Across the country in New York, **IRA** sees the post. Under username ChokeMe83 he answers, "Yes." Then: "I don't want to have to make any decisions anymore. I want someone else to have all the power, and to take care of me."

A chorus of similar sentiments follows, until **ELIOT**, under username AngryCub, replies: "Pussy. Forcing your problems on someone else."

Lorrie believes in freedom of speech, so she lets the comment stay. She types: "Why are you so angry, @AngryCub?

Rather than replying publicly in the thread, AngryCub private messages her a couple hours later. The length of his rant suggests that he's spent most of the time in between writing it. Beneath his anger, Lorrie recognizes the truer tones of grief. She hears a young man feeling confused and quite alone and she thinks she can relate to the isolation. "Listen," she responds. "There's something I think you should see."

The link that Lorrie sends to Eliot opens up on an envelope. Gold lettering sparkles on a background almost sumptuous in its blackness.

Dear Lorrie,

The problem is that every time I try to demonize Ira, I feel like the freak. Everything about me—this body, this self—feels wrong. I look at other people and see how they are happy and I am not happy and I cannot think of a single thing that would make me so. This body isn't mine. This life isn't mine. I don't remember choosing it and I know I'm supposed to want it. But I don't, Lorrie. I don't.

-El

Dear Eliot,

I wish I could give you a hug. Let's meet next time I'm in New York.

-Lorrie

Dear Lorrie,

That would be nice. If I live that long. Quite frankly, I don't much see the point in it all these days.

-El

Dear Eliot,

Today I was walking through the park and I saw a large old house all decorated for Halloween. Synthetic cobwebs plastered the porch and faux tombstones shook in the breeze. I tried to imagine your name on one of them and it made me really sad. I hope you'll reconsider, at least until we can meet—and then I'll convince you in-person.

-Lorrie

Dear Lorrie,

Halloween is my favorite holiday. I love the warm colors, the cool air, and the sense of possibility infusing everything. You're right. I need to see another Halloween. How do you feel about haunted houses?

-El

Dear Eliot,

I adore haunted houses. I like not knowing what's around every corner, and feeling the fear of anticipation even when there's really nothing to be afraid of. I love how people become other people when they're wearing masks. It frees them of responsibility, and the burden of being themselves. Have you tried it?

-Lorrie

Dear Lorrie,

The spine is a colorful organic structure through which energy and motion shiver. There is no place for moderation in the relationship between reason and passion, excess and restraint.

Fate, fortune, and chance are Greek gods meddling in Greek lives. No one alive is free. We are slaves to concepts that keep us from acting on our own good sense. Hecuba slaughtered thousands of tiny sit-on-your-lap children. If you know you're going to fail, why try?

-El

Dear Eliot,

One must earn the right to violence.

-Lorrie

Dear Lorrie,

Catharsis doesn't work in psychosis because there's no loss.

-El

"Say 'ahh,'" **CAPTAIN HOOK** instructs, depressing Lorrie's tongue. Her tongue has most recently been wrapped around his cock. "Yeah," he says, "I can see it. Your tonsils are swollen like whoa."

"What kind of disease are you carrying anyway?" Lorrie accuses.

"I'm clean as a whistle," Bartholomew replies. "You're the one with the nasty case of strep."

"So, what—you can prescribe meds, too?"

"I'll hook you up, no problem. But ultimately, those tonsils will have to go."

He shoots her a devious look.

Lorrie understands.

ELIOT takes the office intern out for drinks, then back to his empty apartment.

"I don't like blood," the intern says, as though the statement sums up anything.

It does tell Eliot a few things: for example, he isn't into needle play. But it doesn't rule out ropes. Whips. Pain in general. Does the prospect excite him? Like a fever: hot and chilled at the same time. Like tremors that make the body shake subtly even under a scalding shower.

The intern's aversion to blood also means he isn't into cutting. A vegetarian, he doesn't eat headcheese.

TRICE can't decide when the best time would be to present **FOREST** with his son's new arm. He feels like there should be some fanfare around—some celebration of—Trice's greatest robotic creation yet, and of course the return of Forest's full motor functionality. Should it be on his birthday? Trice wonders. A return to the whole body with which Forest had been born. Or before his birthday, so that he can show off his new arm when he goes out with his friends?

Or what if Forest doesn't like his new arm at all? His son's disappointment would hurt worse than—he almost says Forest losing his arm—but that is a horrible thing to think.

At group, **DON** remembers the days they used to 'play' at war, back when war was a game of strategy with very clear rules and the mortar fire always stopped promptly at dinner time. Even then, Don had always volunteered to be the war amputee, using two long sticks like crutches to hobble around on, his missing leg bent backward and bound heel-to-butt cheeks. The uncommon proclivity had earned him the nicknames 'gimp' and 'wannabe' long before anyone knew that an amputee-in-training is in fact called a wannabe. That's what Don had been: an amputee in training. He'd become an amputee for real the very next summer.

Baby lambs are less innocent than 10-year-old boys. American fifth grade males have already peaked in terms of intelligence, but are largely unconcerned yet with girls. Their bodies may react, but their minds don't know why. Nocturnal vixens (likely looking like mom) vanish with the dawn, a dampness to the sheets the only evidence the wet dream ever was real.

By the same reasoning, when the Allies took over new territory in Springfield, everything that followed was an autonomic (i.e. unconscious) response.

Little Don is the RTO (radio telephone operator). He falls in line behind the company commander and the point man. They creep, slowly and silently, to the first checkpoint, where they relieve the first platoon's security detail.

As the skies begin to sprinkle, the boys move into ambush patrol position. They enter Cooper's Woods, a thicket of trees that stretch 40 feet tall and hundreds of acres wide. The trees are like umbrellas, sheltering the GIs from the rain and blotting out the blue of the sky. Ensconced in shadow while it is yet early evening, the loudest sounds are the wind and the boys' labored breathing. They keep one hand on their weapons, and one tucked into the ammo belt of the boy in front of him, moving like an articulated snake through the underbrush.

Just then, the FO (forward observer) turns his ankle stepping into a hole. He falls to the ground, gritting his teeth and trying not to whimper. The convoy can't stop for anything, so Don steps around him and becomes the point man.

A cracking twig to the left, and the boys see that the enemy has been waiting for them to walk into their trap. Charlie company hits the deck, hands instinctively grappling for slingshots. Don takes a rock to the shoulder. He groans and slumps to the ground. It's hard to work a slingshot with just one good hand.

He tries to signal to the medic: A little help over here! But the medic is busy attending to a boy who took a rock to the head. The bullet blasted through his helmet, ricocheted round, and left his skull looking like a messily-cracked egg. He's a goner. The medic should leave him and attend to the boys who still have a chance.

Suddenly, the *blatblatblat* of a chopper can be heard overhead. Dust-off has come for them; they're aborting the mission! Don army-crawls back toward the clearing where the chopper will attempt to land. Rain and mud in his eyes, he moves blindly, planting one elbow in front of himself at a time and dragging his torso bodily along.

Consequently, he never sees the ancient steel jaws of the long-rusty animal trap into which he feeds his leg like a sacrifice. The 10-year-old weighs just enough to trigger the spring. It snaps. It takes a bite of Don.

The pain has a color, and that color is electric white. The clean neon of an alien ship's beam maybe. Futuristic. Sharp. Terrifying and intriguing at the same time. An honor to be one of the Chosen Ones.

Because it has been raining, the small dampness that darkens the front of Don's pants is indistinguishable from the muck and the mire. His deep, soul-wracking sigh might indicate shock—or the singular pleasure of enlightenment, followed by the crash. Having eaten but once from the Tree of Knowledge, the aftermath is always a bit of existential dread. Attended by tetanus. Accompanied by amputation.

I'm attracted to anything with two legs. Or one leg. Or the girl I met on Tindr. She had one arm. She was hot.

Where did her arm end specifically? Did she tell you the story?

I didn't ask. We talked about how most gay bars in Europe are for men (as opposed to gay women).

Are missing limbs more common in gay bars?

I have no idea. She seemed very confident, which was intimidating.

Confidence comes from loving who you are and believing you can do anything.

Exactly! That's what made her so attractive.

What body part would you like to be rid of? Or if none, what could you live without?

Ears, I think.

Why did van Gogh cut off his ear? Is a hysterectomy an amputation? How do you feel about dogs with docked tails?

We had a dog with a tail that curled. In all 3 questions I'm thinking about power. Who has the most power? Are they abusing it?

What if the person wants to be powerless?

Might being powerless actually cultivate a sense of power?

Perhaps being powerless would confirm one's power over oneself, given that to willingly give up power would take (I imagine) a lot of self-control. But the desire to be powerless could also stem from a lack of self-esteem.

On the contrary, I imagine that wanting to be powerful comes from not believing in one's self. How do power dynamics come into play with amputation fetishes?

In a similar way, though typically the effects are more permanent. I once read about a woman who had her boy-friend cut off her last knuckle on one finger. It was erotic every time she looked at it—maybe in the same way that seeing a strap-on would affect other people.

Is the fetish community large? Underground? Do people feel that they are defined by their fetishes?

Fairly underground, yes, but quite vocal on the internet. The number of threads I have seen make me think that amputation is not an uncommon fetish after all. As far as being defined, it depends on the person. A gay person can wear rainbow flags all the time and 'advertise,' or disclose his/her orientation only when s/he wants to, right?

Does the anonymity of the internet keep members of the fetish community safe?

Safe from those who would try to physically harm or kill them for their beliefs—but not safe from internet trolls.

The fetish must have existed before the internet. How

*did members find each other before there were online forums?
Newspaper ads?*

Do body parts matter?

Silence.

GEORGE wakes just before dawn. He stares unmoving at the stars for a time, lost in the Milky Way's majesty, before coming back to where and who and why he is.

Soft sounds slowly penetrate night's velvet curtain. Chirping insects. A northerly wind. The swaying sage. An inaudible warmth that nevertheless seems to groan from the ground, originating from somewhere near the fire's popcorn-popping embers.

George can hear these subtle rabbit songs because the ringing has stopped. For once in his terrible twilit years the incurable, insufferable tinnitus has been cured, no longer causes him to suffer.

Monica.

Propping himself up on one elbow, George looks around for his savior. Nihimá has departed, but left George under the protective charms of the thick Navajo blanket, the necklace of knotted talismans.

When George trusts his legs again, he stands. Slowly.

He heads toward home (the direction the sun will rise) and he rejoices in the scuffing sigh of his footfalls in the Arizona desert.

There's a magic to gardens that stretch forever. Like seas that have finally been tamed. Close-cropped grassy green fields welcome the casual stroller by day and camouflage the faun's footprint by night. The gardens smell of bougainvillea; the macarons they serve there taste like rose petals. In the heart of the labyrinth, fish bake on a pedestal in the sun, having swallowed one too many cigarette butts.

MONICA walks out among the roses. The ground is damp yet with dew, even though the day has grown well into the afternoon, for the patch of grass she chooses to sit on lays perpetually in shadow.

She watches the people around her. The environment through which they all move. Mostly they sit in pairs: friends or partners. Seven turtles sun themselves on a rock. Even the statues are engaged in conversation. Soldier and slave. Nymph and amorous escort. The sun shines as warm as it ever does in Denmark, which is to say it is a summer day that has peaked at a state of 'pleasant,' absent Arizona's burning sear. Plus she can sit on the soft grass without fear of a fire ant bite (or several).

She could use a vodka lemonade. Or at the very least,

a purpose. With the latest case closed, 'relaxing' feels like wasted time unsanctified by productivity (and therefore prosperity). She wonders if all the solo young men around her are university students. They all read their books intently, and chain-smoke absentmindedly. Are years leaving their lives as she watches? Or is an early death that silences a brain full of too many ideas the ideal? Why does her hair keep falling in her face? Why had she been unable to reschedule her flight? Why is she alone? Why does it feel like the fairytale died with HC Andersen?

On Monica's first trip to Europe, she had arrived at CDG airport with completely unrealistic and over-romanticized expectations of the city. Having watched and fallen in love with Woody Allen's *Midnight in Paris*,[64] she had scoured the streets for those intimate but uncrowded candlelit cafes, secret jazz clubs, and gentlemen's cabarets. Between consulting sessions, she had scanned the sky for the Eiffel Tower. Wished to walk where Dali, Picasso, Gertrude Stein, and Hemingway had smoked, sipped cocktails, and made their art. What she'd found instead was a world too small. Paris had been infected with tourists as with lice: their white and brown bodies crawled over each other in grimy gutters, paying exorbitant rates for bottled water and souvenir berets. Stood in line for hours for experiences that lasted five minutes. Fell over themselves to propose at the top of the Tower, before clinking flutes of champagne from Reims that sold for 20x their value. Those 'cute' cafes had been choked with clouds of BO and cigarette smoke. Because the waitstaff didn't work for tips like they did in the United States, service had been slow, leaving Monica to languish and marinate in the foul concoction.

Copenhagen is better, though she has little hope

[64] A 2011 American-French romantic comedy film.

that it will produce a dark and brooding Pierre either. Monica had stopped looking for magic in Paris and tried to come to terms with the fact that there were far too many people, wifi hotspots, and bad macarons (come on, no one likes black licorice flavor) to any longer be the 1920 City of Lights and late-night laughter, the Foxtrot and the Fitzgeralds. In Denmark she banishes all hopes of a European love to the noisy depths of the metro, where they belong.

It's really too bad about Pierre. She needs a fuck.

Convinced that her server is never coming back, Monica finally just leaves a 20 Euro note on the table to cover her coffee and croissant, and skedaddles. She wanders down Strøget, toward the Nyhavn canal, window-shopping a string of galleries as she goes. When she sees the sculpture of a girl-child with a pile of pink earthworms where her head should be, she steps inside the gallery for a closer look. The piece is charming and grotesque at the same time: what kid doesn't play with worms in the dirt? (But what kid has her head devoured by them?)

The sculpture stands on its own columnar pedestal, and as Monica leans in to admire the detail in the segmented bodies, the unexpected voice of the artist she hadn't noticed nearly sends her flying into the sculpture. "Oh, sorry!" **ODYSSEIA** says, an apologetic grin on her face. "I didn't mean to startle you."

"That's alright. Are you the sculptor then?"

"I am. My name is Odysseia Banes. I'd shake your hand, but, well …"

And now it is Monica's turn to offer an awkward smile. Odysseia has no arms. At all. The chiffon sleeves of her aquamarine blouse are knotted at her shoulders. The question that hangs between them is obvious: how exactly does Odysseia sculpt?

As if she'd asked the question aloud, Odysseia says, "I'll show you."

The artist sits on a round stool before a giant block of clay. Slipping off her sandals, she raises her feet like they are hands to the end table that waits next to the clay, and with her toes deftly grabs a sponge and an instrument that looks like a thick wooden tongue depressor. The sponge she dips into a small bucket of water, squeezing it between two toes to wring out the excess. Then she applies it to the clay mound, leaving smooth, glistening swatches of clay everywhere she swabs. Finally, cradling the block with the leg that still grips the sponge, Odysseia brings her right foot, tongue depressor at the ready, to the prepared surface. She pushes the tool into the clay repetitively with sure, quick motions that leave regular impressions.

"Goin' nowhere fast, eh?" Monica jokes—then immediately regrets her own poor taste.

"If you want fast food art," Odysseia replies evenly, "go to Hobby Lobby."

And with that, Monica pulls up a stool next to the woman and watches her work. For hours.

They talk the whole time. No one else comes into the gallery to bother them. Instead Monica wanders around, inspecting and admiring individual sculptures, each one more surreally interesting than the last. When she sees the mass of war-torn bodies writhing just like the girl-child's worms, she smiles and bends to look closer. Yes, those are Union brass buttons embedded in the soldiers' ceramic jackets. "Are they real?" she asks Odysseia.

"They're real."

"How'd they end up in Denmark?"

"Everything is for sale."

"You know, I have a friend who works at a Civil War museum in the States. I know she'd love to borrow this piece, create an exhibit around it. Do you have any more on the same theme?"

"War?" Odysseia scoffs. "Every piece I make is an act of war."

The praying mantis stares back as intently as **TRICE** stares at it, mesmerized perhaps by its own reflection in the engineer's designer eyeglasses. Does the mantis see its own bulbous, multifaceted eyes looking into its soul, or Trice's eyes studying its body, looking for evidence of a soul? Searching in the beheading tendencies of the female for the reason why a species might destroy itself—because then he might understand why mankind goes to war with and for but against other men, honor somehow bound up in killing the enemy, but never eating him. Native peoples ate or used the whole buffalo; only the white man killed for sport. The mantis kills but does not eat its mate. Chimpanzees kill and sometimes eat their kin. Which is closer to the truth? The food chain that puts man at the top but God even higher—in charge of the marionette strings—absolving us from culpability—despite the Church's best attempts to keep us guilty—on our knees—praying to the invisible puppeteer in the sky—because lying is a thing now, having also been invented by man.

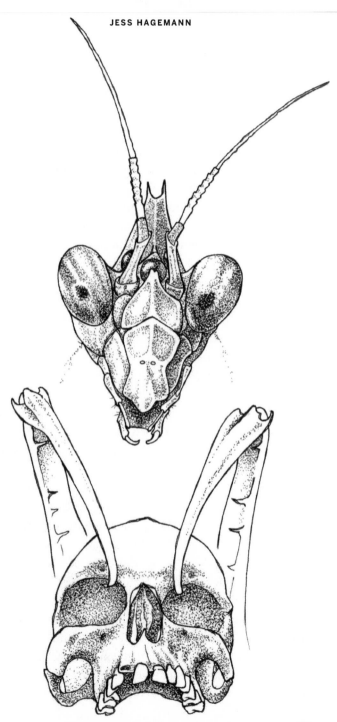

They can't find **RALPH** anywhere. He wouldn't have just not shown up at the site, not without calling or nominating a replacement. He wouldn't have just not used his cell phone or credit cards for nearly three weeks. Would not have abandoned the comfortable home with its mismatched but comfortable furniture: all those well-worn couch cushions and thick wooly blankets meant to combat the Midwestern winter while keeping heating costs low. Would not have walked out on a loyal dog that loved Ralph more than anyone (the feeling was mutual), leaving the door open as he left, letting Grover out to roam the streets and scavenge Springfield's trash. "He just wouldn't do it, they say. Something must have happened. Maybe he was kidnapped?" But who would kidnap a lower-middle class construction site manager? (And in Springfield, no less, where nothing exciting ever happened beyond the occasional racial tension—but Ralph was white.) *Maybe he's on drugs? Maybe he pissed off his dealer?* There'd been no needles, spoons, or wrapping papers at 1113 East Avenue. Not even an errant leaf of dried tobacco. "No, he's clean," his majority Hispanic workers had insisted. "Mr. Ralph doesn't even drink coffee!"

What they don't know about, and so never think to ask about, are the nightmares that plague Ralph's waking moments. His support group members would have understood. They all share the bad dreams that leave them shaking in cold sweats at night: dreams of lost limbs and the occasional decapitation. Ralph is the best listener that any of them have ever known. He never judges, or censures, or tells them they are messed up. "Thank you for sharing," he always says humbly and without pretense. "This is a safe space, and I'm glad you feel safe with us."

The group knows, too, that Ralph mourns the loss of a limb. A part that while unseen, is nevertheless vital to his functioning as a whole human being, and for which there can be no prosthetic. No matter how advanced artificial limb technology becomes, no lightweight, virtually-indestructible system of rods, pulleys, and clamps could ever mend the raw and gaping wound where **LORRIE** lives. His daughter. His own precious beating heart.

The first successful heart transplant was performed in 1967. Its recipient died 18 days later from double pneumonia, contracted when immunosuppressants (administered to keep the man's body from rejecting the new heart) worked a little too well. As anti-rejection drugs have improved, heart transplants have become more common. The biggest problem now is finding enough suitable donors. In 2016, 22 Americans died every day waiting for a new heart.

Ralph understands that when the heart fails, there's no fixing it. It's not heartache he feels, because his heart has been taken from him. It's more an empty pit of nothingness that slowly he's been filling with rage. His daughter's mother had taken Lorrie one evening while he was at group, leaving nothing but one of the girl's days-of-the-week socks—a Tuesday—(which is how he knows it was a Tuesday when his heart stopped beating) lying on on the ground, having slipped so carelessly out of his life. Taking Ralph's life with her.

That's why, the day that Ralph finally snaps, he leaves his home. Leaves the dog. Leaves one bar only to enter another. Because he'd been left behind, and needed now to go after what was his. What had been taken from him. Needed to find his heart as no transplant would do. No prosthetic—human, pig, or machine—could cauterize the vessels. He'd simply bleed out. And so he'd left, either to find Lorrie or to curl up in the woods and die.

Blackout drunk, Ralph falls into a snowbank and

passes out. He sleeps all through the evening, somehow surviving temperatures as low as 20 degrees. When the magazine stand proprietor finds Ralph next to his stall the following morning, first he checks to make sure the man is still breathing. It is while gripping Ralph's wrist to feel for a pulse that **XIOMARA**'s son notices the graying fingers. Frostbite. The stand owner has never seen it before, but all the same he is sure. Those fingers are coming off. And maybe (though he can't see them inside the leather work boots) the toes are, too.

After feeling for a pulse, **MR. D**. feels for his cell phone. He pats all his pockets, wasting what he's convinced are precious seconds, trying to locate the damn thing. It's in his jacket's breast pocket. He fumbles taking it out. Dialing the numbers 911 should be no problem. His gloves have the fingertips cut off, exposing the pads of his thumbs. Even so, it's so cold that Mr. D. struggles to make his thumbs move right, to perform the functions that his mind is telling them to. He'd heard that at the current temperature, one should limit one's exposure to ten minutes outside. Who knows how long the construction site manager has been outside. Who knows how he is still alive.

Mr. D. finally presses the call button. A 911 operator finally answers. Mr. D. describes the unconscious man's state, and gives her the address of his stand. Then because there is no reason for Mr. D to keep suffering, he unlocks his booth and goes inside. He flips on the generator. Hears the heater start to do its thing. Presses brew on the tiny coffee pot he keeps in the tiny kitchen, then sticks his head back out to check on Ralph. It's 4:40 on a Monday morning. The city was as quiet as it ever is, and Mr. D. thinks maybe that siren he hears in the distance is headed their way.

In the interim, Mr. D. isn't sure what to do. He asks

the operator, who tells him to remain on the line. *Should I move him? Bring him inside my booth? Should I put my gloves on his hands?*

The operator advises against moving an unconscious person. "You can put the gloves on him," she says, "but it's likely too late." What good could they do anyway, he thinks, with the fingertips cut off?

When the coffee pot quits perking, Mr. D. fills two ceramic mugs with the steaming brown liquid. He takes the first outside to Ralph, and sets it gently on the man's barely-moving chest. He takes the construction site manager's hands, now wearing Mr. D.'s gloves, and wraps them around the mug, where they stay as if he's fallen asleep that way. Mr. D. hopes the warmth of the coffee might radiate through the mug. Might draw some blood back into Ralph's pale hands.

That's how the paramedics find him: a sad almost-corpse holding coffee like a bouquet of funeral flowers or the rosary in a Catholic nun's hands. They set the coffee on the ground before setting Ralph on a stretcher, and they thank Mr. D. for calling in the case.

It is 4:52 when the ambulance drives away. At 5:00, Mr. D. opens his stand. His buddy, who sells cigarettes next door, raps his signature knock on the back of Mr. D.'s booth. He's come looking for coffee, as is their morning ritual.

Mr. D. kicks the back door open with his foot, and Mr. B. pokes his head in to the kitchen to see Mr. D. rinsing out "his" mug. "What, you been entertaining others in here now?" Mr. B. asks, mock-offended.

Mr. D. declines to engage. He refills the re-rinsed ceramic mug and hands it to the very alive man with winter-red fingers. The fingers take it, gratefully, and Mr. B. smiles.

Across town, at Wade Memorial hospital, Ralph's hands are turned into Mr. D.'s gloves. Which is to say, his fingers are snipped off, each at the first knuckle, using what looks like a pair of surgical steel bolt-cutters. The construction site manager's feet are not so lucky. He loses not only the toes, but midway up his left arch, and all the way to his right ankle. The doctors hadn't revived him before they began the surgery: the threat of gangrene as the tissue warmed to room temperature had been too serious. So Ralph awakes without a job, and without his feet. He'll never leave fingerprints again.

In the years after the Nazi death camps were shut down, the UK was awarded one million pounds by Germany's government to distribute as remuneration to death camp survivors. Of the 4,000-odd British citizens to initially qualify, only about 1,000 of them ever saw any money. The interview process was long and arduous, and some ex-prisoners were questioned for years only to never receive any payment at all.

Among those who did: Tal Ritzenberg, 20£ for the loss of a finger. How Tal lost the finger is unknown.

Better documented is the extensive cannibalism that occurred in camps like Bergen-Belsen.[65] (Seriously: what is with Germany and cannibalism?) As one survivor put it: "At night, it was kill or be killed. By day, eat or be eaten. And maybe eaten anyway if you'd been killed the night before." Food was scarce and the bodies were plentiful. Until the war finally ended, there was only one way out of the camps: through the chimney.

No one except Neo-Nazis today extol the virtues of the German army. What they did to the Jews and others—what they as good as forced the Jews and others to do to their own—begs no forgiveness. Ever.

But what about when consensual amputation—and later, cannibalism—does breed celebrity? Might it encourage copycat killers the way that, say, school shootings do in America?

---

[65] The camp was liberated on April 15, 1945, by the British 11th Armoured Division.The soldiers discovered approximately 60,000 prisoners inside, most of them half-starved and seriously ill, and another 13,000 corpses lying around the camp unburied. The horrors of the camp, documented on film and in pictures, made the name "Belsen" emblematic of Nazi crimes in general in the immediate post-1945 period.

First there was Miewes. Then Japan's Issei Sagawa[66] stepped up to the plate. Like Miewes, he was never convicted of murder. Unlike Miewes, he managed to escape even a manslaughter charge. Before his case was ever tried, Sagawa was declared insane—mentally unfit to stand trial. Despite his own point-blank confession to killing, raping the corpse of, and then dismembering and eating fellow Sorbonne classmate Renée Hartevelt, not enough hard evidence could be found to convict Sagawa. He was remanded to a Japanese mental institution for awhile, before checking out on his own recognizance.

At which point Sagawa's story should have faded into relative obscurity. Instead, treating him like a real-life Hannibal Lecter,[67] the local cops began consulting Sagawa on other murder cases, seeking insight into the minds of other madmen. Sagawa not only played along, he relished the limelight that his involvement trained back upon himself, and milked his 'celebrity' for all it was worth. News spots followed, then exclusive interviews, and finally a string of book deals. These fictional accounts were but thinly-veiled recountings of the Hartevelt murder, describing with graphic detail the way a woman's flesh looks as it is cut, what it tastes like—and importantly, which parts taste the best.

Through it all and to this day, Sagawa remained and remains a free man. He walks the streets alongside you and me. But don't worry. He's expressed remorse over killing Renée, saying "I wish I could have eaten her while she was still alive." Death is not really his bag. When his time comes, however, Sagawa wants to be killed by a woman. To in fact drown in a pool of her saliva.

---

[66] A Japanese author and reviewer who in 1981, while in Paris, murdered and cannibalized a Dutch woman named Renée Hartevelt.

---

[67] A character in a series of suspense novels by Thomas Harris.

LORRIE orders ox tongue sliders off a happy hour menu, thinking 'ox tongue' a fancy name for a strange cut of meat. She never for a second considers that it might actually be the tongue of an ox. But there are the taste buds dotting the thick slab of muscle like so much goose-flesh. She flashes back to Grandpa's cows: the way they'd accepted handfuls of hay from her child's fist, then licked her palm with rough, wet tongues.

When Lorrie takes a bite of the slider, she tries not to picture making out with a cow. Tries not to think about French kissing or other French things since suddenly the cow that the tongue belonged to has become very French in her mind. She notes how the tongue is chewy. Juicy.

And she's tasting her own tongue now. Yes. Chewy. Juicy.

Third she tastes the onions on the toasted artisan bun, and the spices in which the tongues have been baked.

Tongue? Tongues? How big is one beef tongue and how many sliders might it produce? There are three sliders in Lorrie's red and white waxed paper boat. They cost $6. $2/slider. $2 for a piece of taste-budded tongue.

If man meat was sold in grocery stores to canni-bal-happy campers like Miewes and Sagawa, what would it sell for? What would the market support and the people demand? If the test offerings didn't sell, would it be remaindered for dog food? Would dogs develop a taste for human alongside beef and chicken? And why is beef called beef and not cow? And why is chicken called chicken and not poultry? And what would human meat be called? Homo? Are we red meat or white meat? Dark thighs or light? Would our fat content be ground into quantifiable percentages? Would some of us go on sale? Hormone-free? Antibiotic-free? Cage-free? Would it only be on a voluntary basis, like organ donation? Who would regulate the industry? The FDA? The AMA? God forbid, the NSA? Would human livers, if not suitable for donation, be sold on a shelf next to chicken livers? Would they use us for fish food? What if fish developed a taste for human? Imagine the fish in those Thai tourist traps that eat the dead skin off your toes suddenly eating your toes.

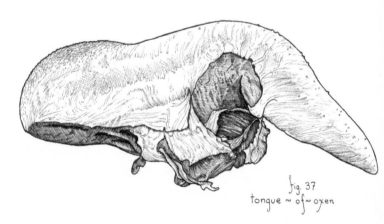

fig. 37
tongue ~ of ~ oxen

In February, Lorrie finally realizes who the tall blond is that squeezes through the tiny door in her dreams: it's **SANTA SANGRE**—Saint Blood—the holes where arms used to be spouting gore like a Jodorowsky[68] film, only she's completely intact, perfectly whole, the only wetness teasing from.behind.within the closed lips of her smile. The stickier lips between her legs occasionally dripping dew onto Lorrie's body below—body and bread. Blood the transference, the transubstantiation of foodstuffs into redemption. Cue Cannibal Holocaust.[69] Cue Oates' Zombie.[70] Q__ P__ creating a legion of zombies with ice pick lobotomies: young men to lick, suck, and spread their cheeks and say, "Thank you, Master; I love you, Master."

But Santa Sangre wants willful subservience. A goddess who has come to expect obeisance, she was born from the fountains of Versailles's royal gardens where luxury is a way of life. Despite Lorrie's average life—her normal, boring, middle-class life: single-woman-in-young-adulthood-still-trying-to-find-herself life—Santa Sangre sees in Lorrie everything she is becoming. The day will come when Lorrie ascends to the throne that like some director's chair already has her name on it. Until then, Hannah keeps kissing Lorrie's neck, leaving burn marks everywhere she touches. Her whole, non-amputated Santa Sangre arms more like Saint Blaze[71] than Saint Blood, blessing Lorrie's throat with her fire.

If she stops to think about it, Lorrie might use the word 'possessed' to describe the way her nocturnal fanta-

[68] A Chilean-French film and theatre director, screenwriter, playwright, actor, author, poet, producer, composer, musician, comics writer, and spiritual guru.

[69] A 1980 English-language Italian cannibal exploitation horror film directed by Ruggero Deodato from a screenplay by Gianfranco Clerici.

[70] A 1995 novel by Joyce Carol Oates based on the life of Jeffrey Dahmer.

[71] Saint Blaise; a physician, and bishop of Sebastea in historical Armenia.

sy life has overtaken and blended with her waking reality. By day, the internet is a portal to research, so as to understand, the stranger things she didn't know she needed.

The invitation arrives like all the others: a hidden Bitly link. A velvet black envelope. Gold lettering promising the most cathartic show yet: freedom through exorcism—through the excision of parasitic parts.

In a small Wisconsin town, a woman with a boyfriend leaves the boyfriend behind to spend a day with John and Bloody Ruckus. They drink nothing alcoholic and they do no drugs but drinking comes up anyway. Blood-drinking. Bloody Ruckus suggests that the woman allow him to cut her arm with a blade. Collect her blood in a shot glass. He will drain the shot in one gulp.

That's what happens.

Appetite whetted, Bloody Ruckus next suggests that blood alone is not enough. With the woman's permission, he pins down her hand. Uses a machete to chop her pinky off flush with her palm. He drops the finger in a plastic baggy and puts it in the freezer. He will eat it later, he says.

That's what happens.

Although **BARTHOLOMEW 'CAPTAIN HOOK' JORDAN** specializes in clean, creative 'corrections' to the human body, **DON** doesn't know that Bartholomew exists the night he decides that the other leg must go. Had he known, Don might've hired Bartholomew for a private session. Instead he hires the neighbor boy.

This is a CHOOSE-YOUR-OWN-ADVENTURE book. Starting now. Because the characters' (your) options should not be limited by the words I write on this page. Black ink. White pages. Same as the drawings. Have you noticed that other stories live in them? I didn't put those there. Chris suggested them and you connected the dots between the plot points. It means you haven't lost your child self's imagination. Which means you're practically a writer. Starting now.

When **SANTA SANGRE** comes through Lorrie's bedroom door—do you slam the door in her face? Erase the chalk lines on the wall that make the door a thing?

When Don makes **CARLOS** chop his leg off for him—do you empathize with Don, or sympathize with Carlos?

Oh wait. That hasn't happened yet.

Carlos is a strapping young man. 17. Strong. More strength than he knows what to do with, really, since Carlos is also (in politically-correct terms) intellectually-challenged. He's slower than a road sign telling drivers to slow. Carlos is also mute. He can't talk, but when he's angry he bellows, tossing people and things around with the bull horns he doesn't have but might as well have, for Carlos is hung like a bull and as randy when he sees something he wants. Sometimes women see Carlos and feel the proverbial stirring of their loins at the way the light picks out his well-developed shoulders, or when imagining how soft his sandy brown hair must be. They mistake his inability to speak for reticence, and then Carlos smiles. When Carlos smiles, his stained and broken teeth, black after years of beatings, leak drool down a chin that no longer seems chiseled but kind of silly, swollen yet with the last of little-boy pudginess. And the gleam the women thought they saw there—it's an animal's leer. Hungry and understanding nothing but instinct. Fear. Desire.

So what do you do? Promise to jump Carlos's bones with a come-hither finger wag? Or start shrieking, calling for the cops, grabbing for the nearest frying pan as, suddenly thrown into an unthinking fit, refraining only that the 'stupid, rabid beast must die,' you swing wildly but connect anyway, Carlos too t-u-r-t-l-e slow to duck?

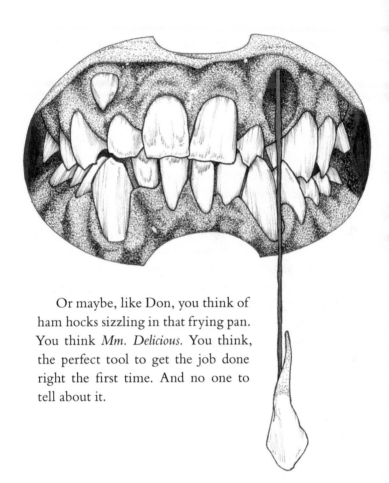

Or maybe, like Don, you think of ham hocks sizzling in that frying pan. You think *Mm. Delicious.* You think, the perfect tool to get the job done right the first time. And no one to tell about it.

Don spots Carlos over the rim of his coffee mug one early Saturday morning. Steam rises from the mug before his eyes and he blinks them rapidly, as though to clear from vision this impossible Michelangelo. When Carlos doesn't disappear—is, in fact, real—Don takes in Carlos's flannel shirt and dirty blue jeans, his well-worn boots and his baby blue eyes. Don dunks a fresh apple-cinnamon donut in his coffee and feels the wet, warm mass enter his mouth like a soft, warm cock. He chews, and watches Carlos move between the farmers' market booths. Don watches the cowboy eye Don's wife's pies longingly. He watches **PETUNIA** pink up as she also watches Carlos, oblivious to Don, her husband of 35 years. Her (secretly) bitter and (completely) closeted husband: a war vet who never talks about those days with her, but who so nobly leads a support group every week in downtown Springfield. She doesn't know that Don has never seen war, like she doesn't even suspect that he's gay. Like she has no fucking idea that Don dreams of being a triple amputee. Or that Carlos will be the pawn to make it happen.

Don approaches. "Damn good pies," he says, nodding at Petunia's most popular—strawberry rhubarb.

When Carlos pulls out his wallet, Don claps him on one bony shoulder. "Damn good choice, son." (Pause.) "My name's Don."

You're Carlos. Do you smile a snaggletoothed smile and eat your pie? Do you gore Don with your invisible bull horns, confident from the way he touches you that the act would be one of self-defense?

Across the corridor of white-tented booths, **FOREST**, **TRICE**'s son, scans the crowd for Carlos. *I knew I should've leashed him with the others*, Forest thinks, eying the three unfortunates bound wrist-to-wrist with Forest's one good wrist so they can't wander and get lost. Carlos had promised with a puppy-dog nod to stay by Forest's side. And now he's lost in a land of fruits.

Oh, there he is! Talking to Don! Shoving his piehole with, well, pie.

Remove any one bone and the body continues functioning. Connective tissue holds the skeleton in place. Organs prop each other up like bean bags.

What if one day the spleen fell into the foot?

And stayed there. And its charger cord kept it plugged in and working. But it flattened a little under the weight-bearing heel. Providing great cushion for bunions. Soothing plantar fasciitis. In addition to all the normal functions of the spleen, like filtering out damaged red blood cells and producing new white blood cells. Would the spleen then be more or less susceptible to laceration? It wouldn't slam into the seat belt in a car accident, but a too-hard kick of the soccer ball? Risky.

And didn't Freud talk like spleen was a condition of melancholy.

And didn't ancient Egypt rehouse the spleen in canopic jars.

And doesn't the spleen work in tandem with the pancreas.

And doesn't spleen like liver taste dark red and gummy at dinner.

And doesn't Dottie come back for her stolen liver, while no ghost ever pined for spleen?

And does amputation only imply cutting? What about gouging? Will you donate your corneas at death, feel the slice-amputation of a layer removed?

Will you spoon-gouge the whole eye, dropping it unceremoniously like a cherry on your chocolate ice cream? Swallowing it whole then puking it back up, only to say "I need to get her out of me." Reverse-birthing parts that won't be reattached, their owner long-digested.

On Sunday I mistake the athlete standing there casually, hip thrust forward cockily, left arm planted on left hip (out of sight), for a bro. Not crouched, and apparently not ready to receive, he looks unprepared for the volleyball served streamlined and whistling. No way that he will feel without seeing the ball smack extended forearms held taut just so, swinging then stopping just so, to bump to waiting setter in perfect body-calculated arc. Feet buried in the sand, black crickets raining from four floodlights, I judge him lazy.

But ball sails to athlete and athlete brings one arm (his right) forward to pop the ball up like an underhand serve. His right arm is not joined by his left arm because the athlete's left arm was one time reduced to a pile of ashes, incinerated at the medical waste facility alongside aborted fetuses and stool samples discarded via the garbage chute at Wade Memorial Hospital.

Did you know that ashes are pulverized bone? Only the bones survive the burning. Not clothes. Not skin. Not the very marrow heat-sucked and susceptible to flame. Only the bones are pulverized, and I like to picture giant mortar, giant pestle, giants grinding those bones to make their bread. When ashes are scattered on the beach, across the waves, fish and seagulls eat the specks as though they are bread—the specks sterile until the salt of the ocean. Then accumulating life. Growing a fur of green algae. Sinking perhaps or swept through the baleen of some hulking, plankton-eating whale. The giant of the sea. Hanging out in aquatic fields of gently-waving sea stalks like beanstalks, only less legumish, more air-light bubble pods and salt.

Did you know that both beans and seaweed convert nitrogen? Store minerals? Look green or brown or black or white depending on time of day, on the density of pollutants?

The athlete with one arm gives a half-fumbled return, the ball striking broadside a forearm canted inward. Setter wiggles himself beneath the ball, corrects return. Sends a high one out and skyward. A strong-side hitter approaches as set is still ascending. Jumps as ball begins descending. Swings at the instant that 9.8 g/s of gravitational force position ball at spiker's palm and S L A M S the thing directly into net.

Ricocheting.

Hitting no one's face.

Scoring our team another point.

The net flaps in the non-breeze like the empty sleeve of the athlete's blue t-shirt. Someone says, "It's okay, man." Someone says, "Next time, man."

And the athlete stands cocky-casual again, only this time his stance seems less statement, more adaptation.

The high-pitched ringing starts up again. Walking down Santa Fe's sidewalks or holed up in the Chinle library, the whine is there, drilling deeper into **GEORGE**'s brain. It's the electric buzz of lights and the electromagnetic frequency of wifi and an air conditioning unit that runs through the night in winter—wholly unnecessary but continuing even after George flips the breaker. It's why the offending ears must go. **MONICA** tried but she's gone now to Chicago, not answering George's desperate calls, not opening her door when he pounds insistently upon it at 8 PM, at midnight, at 4 AM.

You don't actually need your outer ear to hear. If there's a piece of the body that can go, it's that one—though not without consequences. The conch shell of the ear is a funnel collecting and directing sound waves to the cochlea. The nerves of the outer ear communicate which direction sound is coming from. A howling coyote. A tinkling strand of fetishes that, hanging from the porch, remind.

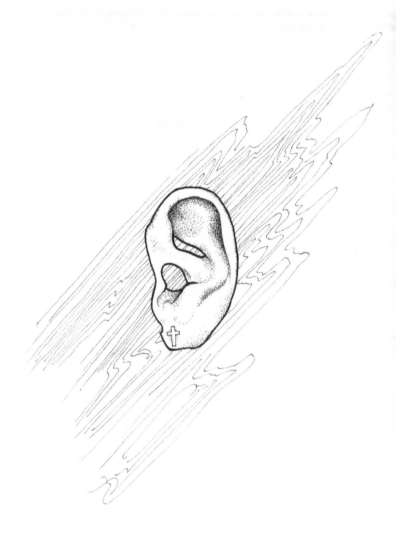

All the tall, beautiful women parade past in black lace, baring various degrees of cleavage and midriff, lining the perimeter of the room. All of them look like **HANNAH** and all of them are **LORRIE**, each a different her in a different world where she chose differently, where the lives in the rooms she moved through evolved differently, and so they are not quite her, either. Betrayed by new smile lines, dimples, and freckles, tattoos and haircuts, boots and stilettos and pedicured or callused bare feet, wine-stained from crushing grapes in Italy, damp from the sucking mouth of a recent lover. They fidget or dance or stand completely still. They are the congregation.

Lorrie, the initiate, enters. Instead of black lace she wears a hospital gown. Barefoot, she pads to the operating table at center stage. Checking to make sure the gurney's wheels are locked, she hops up on it. Straightens her gown. Lies down.

The lights dim save for a mobile light on a moveable arm, the kind above dentists' chairs, that drops now from the ceiling. From the dark periphery, the women begin to hum atonally: the discordant sounds of a pre-show symphony. Some whimper and some crescendo with a shriek. Lorrie, eyes closed, doesn't move. Goes absolutely still.

At the fever pitch of their meowing, the hierophant enters stage left. Only his eyes visible above the surgical mask, below the tufted hair net. Garbed neck to toe in gold and blue robes—and his assistant, too. Nameless. Unimportant.

More important: the flat-screen monitor the assistant wheels ahead of her, the table of instruments she rolls behind her. She snaps the latex gloves on **CAPTAIN HOOK**'s good hand and his better prosthetic hand. She stands aside. Goes absolutely still.

Snapping the latex twice for good measure, Captain Hook begins the tonsillectomy.

In 2016, Texas governor Greg Abbott[72] approves legislation that would mandate the burial or cremation of all aborted or miscarried fetal remains. As if a woman's pain weren't already enough. As though unborn children whose final resting place is a midden or a septic sewer and not consecrated ground will rest any less easy, their tiny frustrated baby fists jerking across time, space, and juju.

The legislation raises questions, of course, and not only the hackneyed *Does life begin at conception?* but *What constitutes life?* and *Where does consciousness reside?* Should the pieces of an obliterated limb prove impossible to reconstruct, can the rest of an incomplete corpse receive a Christian burial? Is a human less human lacking the standard number of limbs? Must the parts lost to frostbite be pulled from the snow like the blood clot pissed into a toilet the morning she awakes aware of having lost some of herself but pretending otherwise? What about the woman who, on entering the clinic, pretends that the inconvenience was never part of herself? An excess to be removed such that the woman can with grateful sigh return to her own whole life?

---

[72] Whellchair-bound, it has been said that Greg Abbott 'stands up for no one.'

GEORGE stands at the yellowed sink in the cramped bathroom of their small southwestern trailer home. Staring back at himself he sees in the vanity mirror a wily long tongue loll out between tobacco-stained teeth, sun-darkened leather lips. His tongue is not black and forked but the pink and lazy tongue of a coyote, ribbed and absurdly strong. George thinks it makes all the sense in the world that Niltsi had placed the most powerful muscle in the body in that foul-smelling saliva pit of the mouth. What does it say about the skills of speech, feeding, kissing, and singing? That these are everything.

He lets out a low croon that trails into a silent howl until uvula may be seen vibrating at back of throat. With long, rough tongue George licks the formica sink, thick with layers of long-gone **SARAH**'s hairspray. Spits out toothpaste that'd built up in sticky gobs, stubbly chin hairs shellacked with age into the finish. Then he rolls his tongue up like a chameleon's.

Taking the safety razor from the cup on the sink, removing blade from razor head, placing blade to Navajo head, depressing. A pinprick of blood blooming. Panting like a dog's.

CAPTAIN HOOK approaches **LORRIE**'s gurney, scissors in right hand (good hand), pointer finger laid lengthwise along the blades for support.control.precision.

And inserting again the tongue depressor (His cock has not been in Lorrie's mouth for 24 hours. It twitches in anticipation.), he inserts a purple felt tip into Lorrie's mouth, past the tongue depressor, to one swollen tonsil. Careful to avoid triggering a gag reflex.

With his other hand, **GEORGE** pulls the top of his right ear away from his head. Stretching cartilage toward mirror, noting without feeling (just a passive observation) the small flecks of waxy yellow buildup in his outer crenula—

211

—while **BARTHOLOMEW** dots a purple-markered line over the white and yellow patches of infection still inflaming the very glands meant to keep **LORRIE** free from infection. The felt tip dabs through pus. Lorrie feels the pressure and the pressure is weird. Nothing usually pressing there except food. Except Bartholomew's cock. But it doesn't make her gag so she keeps her mouth open. Keeps her eyes open. The corners of her eyes streaming now with pain (damn strep) now with the effort of not moving a muscle (damn imperfect body) (soon, very soon, to be made perfect).

Having slipped off his shirt to save it from blood (only **SARAH** had known how to remove blood stains), **GEORGE** touches blade to the back of his ear, at ear-to-scalp joint. He presses and he feels the pressure before the pain. Strange because he's not used to pressure there—maybe only ever before from sunglasses, or the feel of Sarah's mouth as she wrapped around him from behind. Slicing makes no sound, no sound. George moves the blade with intention so that when he is done, no sound, no sound.

So that **LORRIE** doesn't scream but moans, **CAPTAIN HOOK** removes her hospital gown. He pulls one bra cup down and freeing the mound of her breast begins to lick. Suck. Until her back arcs unconsciously. Until Lorrie forgets she isn't alone but on a stage.

There are spectators.

GEORGE never forgets he's alone, his the only reflection in the vanity mirror, cleaving slowly into two.

The growing warmth between **LORRIE**'s legs matches the warm wet cave of her mouth, open now in a little O. It is between these lips with the aid of tongue depressor that **BARTHOLOMEW** inserts the sterile scissors.

GEORGE's razor is far from sterile, but it's sharp. When he's finished tracing ear back, he pulls blade down. against.into the nubbin you press when you want to block out sound. Because for George it has never managed to block out sound, not the ringing. It's a smooth cut, shallow there against the skull, behind the distal end of mandible.

LORRIE's jaw pops once: a tiny escaping pressure as the pressure of blade against tonsil cord finally becomes a severance. She flashes to toes, to the disconnecting of one thing from another. A USB cord from the port. Only power is not lost here but connection made between past and present. Lorrie and **CAPTAIN HOOK**. Lorrie and the strange things that bodies do. She has time to wonder where fetishes come from, to question the blur of a childhood (what, Freud would ask her, happened when you were three?) and then the arch that Bartholomew had put into her back becomes the unspooling of a white hot heat spreading out from somewhere deep in her belly. Bartholomew catches the first tonsil with a strong pair of tongs before it can fall and lodge in Lorrie's throat.

GEORGE doesn't worry about his ears falling off. The outlining complete, connective tissue yet glues cartilage to skull and requires a pulling.sawing.peeling. Something dedicated and intentional.

Setting blade on sink, George takes forefinger and thumb and applies them to ear directly. Gingerly, then with feeling, he pulls the offending appendage. It bows, then pops, finally separating. A letting go.

LORRIE lets go of her control. She winces and groans at the scissors's bite, then marvels at the open space—the feeling of empty where ridged and squishy skin bulb had previously grown. Freed from a burden she'd been born with—

—freed from a burden that had settled on his shoulders with **SARAH**'s death, the ringing a more constant companion than even she had been in life. **GEORGE** drops the ear into the trash without looking at it.

BARTHOLOMEW drops the tonsil into a jar without looking at it. He pinches **LORRIE**'s nipple, hard as a miniature cock.

The hole in the side of **GEORGE**'s head like the entry point of a bullet, or a bleeding Vonnegut asshole.[73] Blood runs copiously as it always does with head wounds.

---

[73] Illustration from *The Breakfast of Champions* (1973).

LORRIE will choke on the blood running down her throat if **BARTHOLOMEW** doesn't cauterize it soon. Choke, and she risks coughing. Cough, and he risks an imprecise second cut. Captain Hook is nothing if not precise with his cuts.

GEORGE grabs the iron from where it's been heating on the lid of the toilet tank, plugged into the outlet that normally charges his electronic toothbrush. He brings it to rest firmly against the side of his face, its metal plate turning blood to steam with a hiss. Shrink-wrapping the wound. Sealed with a sigh.

Quickly subbing heat gun for scissors, **CAPTAIN HOOK** closes **LORRIE**'s attachment point. She shifts on the wheeled bed. One tonsil bobs on the wheeled tray.

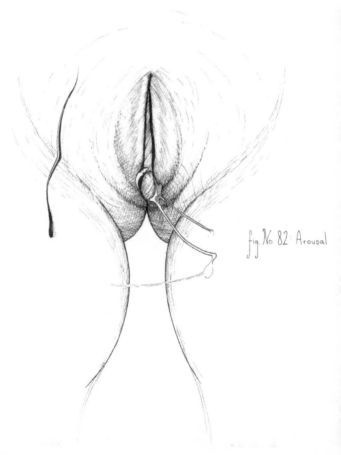

fig. No. 82: Arousal

A Clockwork Orange[74] (the movie version) came out in 1971. EMDR (Eye Movement Desensitization and Reprocessing) wasn't theorized until the '80s, so the only connection between Alex's 'therapy' (you remember, that time he had his eyelids pinned in place?) must have been purely coincidental on Francine Shapiro's[75] part (originating, as all insights do, in the Freudian subconscious). But either way, ten years later she was writing about the effects of eye movement on long-term memory association: how deliberate eye movements (side to side, rapid, like REM) coupled with positive intentions (we'll call them affirmations) could actually rewire the way the brain processes traumatic memories. Turning beliefs like "I am a failure" into "I am successful." Or in the case of veterans, "I am in danger" to "I am safe now." Dissolving deep-seated anger.fear.guilt.

It's a method they try with Captain B. Jordan to little effect and with **FOREST KILLIAN** to significantly more. Both young men have lost an arm. Bartholomew is tormented by the imperfect nubbin that remains: a piece that should have been and must be taken; the pieces of parishioners in his cabaret that should have been and must be taken. Bartholomew feels dirty. No matter how many times he repeats "My body is healthy. It serves me and in serving me my body is perfect," he cannot get beyond 5 or 6 on the Validity of Cognition scale. Only 7 represents true belief; Bartholomew is stuck somewhere in the realm of 'could be but isn't true.' EMDR isn't working for him. His body isn't serving him. So Bartholomew keeps serving others.

Whatever small resentment Forest used to harbor, on

---

[74] Based on Anthony Burgess's 1962 novel of the same name.

[75] An American psychologist and educator who created a form of psychotherapy for reducing the disturbance of negative thoughts and memories.

the other hand, dissolves as he forges new associations between traumatic memory and more adaptive information. Remembering is like repeatedly reinjuring a wound. Remembering causes the wound to fester. For Forest, EMDR therapy removes the block and fosters healing. As his mind goes blank, he feels empowered by what once debased him.

ELIOT is in the audience at **LORRIE**'s tonsillectomy. When he sees Bartholomew pull the bloody glob of throat flesh delicately from Lorrie's mouth, he gets hard and doesn't at first understand why. Does the violence of the moment perhaps remind him of **IRA**? (Ira had made zero effort, by the way, to contact Eliot. Eliot didn't think he would, but still, the sticky threads of hope …)

Or maybe Eliot is viscerally responding to the surgeon's tall, fit body—his utter control over a medical maneuver executed without even breaking a sweat. Bartholomew is undeniably beautiful, but Eliot doesn't think that's it, either. As the discharged army doctor inserts his lighted scope and scissors into Lorrie's mouth a second time, Eliot imagines the taste of the metallic instrument on his own tongue. How cold they must be, then quickly warming to body temperature. Eliot notices how that very sensation makes Lorrie shift a leg on the table, bending one knee involuntarily, revealing for a second the hot place between legs under gown. Eliot's cock jumps in his pants and he gasps audibly. No. He can't possibly be sexually attracted to this person he met on the internet. This … woman. What use had he for a vagina, for the heaving mounds of her breasts rising and falling rapidly.shallowly.hotly beneath hospital-issue garment. Eliot feels arousal and he feels a supreme amount of confusion.

As he watches, his whole lower half becomes a hot pulse, beating in time with a quickening heartbeat. He wants to rush the stage. To fill his mouth with Lorrie's firm tit and lick the length of Captain Hook's pointer finger wrapped just so around the scissors. Lick the man from finger to fuck-wand, to the giant penis he knows must be ready to burst through the good doctor's pants and play! But before he can do anything—even think, really, about moving—Captain Hook pulls the second tonsil free, clasped in the gleaming hug of BBQ tongs, and Eliot comes with the force of a suckerpunch: bent over at the waist in his seat and struggling to breathe.

Revelation floods his understanding like a child tasting honey for the first time. A sweetness thick and pure. A viscous thing to get trapped in.

Eliot is falling down the mineshaft of his own long-boarded-over mind. What lifeforms, sightless and pale, have been evolving down here, waiting so patiently? Can their newly-awakened hunger ever be sated?

With something like horror code-switching halfway across the spectrum to admiration, for the first time ever of his very own accord, Eliot understands what Bartholomew Jordan's therapists had been hoping the captain would accept: that his body is healthy and it serves him well. It is Eliot's turn to serve his body.

For longer than this fangirl would like to admit, Andy Warhol[76] lived with his mother and a couple dozen Siamese cats—all named Sam—in a Pittsburgh apartment. He was convalescing, first as a young adult, later after an assassination attempt that begs the question: what distinguishes assassination from murder? Political or religious motive, I guess. And we all worship at the altar of Edie Sedgwick,[77] the most beautiful woman ever to have lived.

Andy Warhol. Son of Julia Warhola. A printer's error once left the 'a' off of Warhola and Andy gleefully crushed the letter into the ground with the heel of Julia's stiletto on his way to a party, wearing her clothes.

---

[76] An American artist and a leading figure in the visual art movement known as pop art.

---

[77] An American heiress, socialite, actress, and fashion model best known for being one of Andy Warhol's Superstars.

Umbilicus.

After the show, Eliot follows the umbilical cord stretching from his core self to the man on the stage who can make that core a reality.

Dear Ira,

I'm leaving you. I want to say that it's not you, it's me—and it is—but it also, in large part, is you. As a person, you're a bigger prick than the one attached to your body, which is saying something because you are admittedly well-endowed. It's great to have a prick but not so much to be one and recently I have accepted that I deserve better. Better than being talked down to. Used. Or worse—ignored. Better than being your toy without a name—a fucking faceless lover. (When was the last time you looked at me? Really looked at me?) You never noticed my new haircut—I'm styling with pomade these days— or that sometimes I wear colored contacts. Did you really think my eyes were naturally green?

Anyway. I'm not out to 'make you pay,' though the idea has some appeal. (How does one put a 'value' on emotional duress?) I'd say I'd like to hurt you the way you've hurt me, but—I wouldn't really. That's not my style. Especially now that I know so intimately what pain feels like. More than anything I wish I could disappear and pretend like 'we' never happened. Trouble is, I haven't been good at pretending since I was 4. And I don't want to pretend away what I've learned. So that leaves just the disappearing part.

You won't see me again, Ira. Please don't try. (I'm not convinced that you would try—that you even give a single fuck) but if you would, don't. You haven't given me one gift in all the time we've been together. Please grant me this one. It won't cost you anything—not even a second of your jealously-guarded time.

Goodbye, Ira.

In March, **LORRIE** helps to arrange **ODYSSEIA**'s visit to the States. She books her hotel room right next to the museum: a suite on the top floor that overlooks the town. Face pressed to glass, one can see beyond the window quaint cobblestone streets and ancient oaks interrupted at every other corner with a big bank building or chain restaurant slowly choking the few remaining independent retailers and cafes. Midwest winters mean heavy gray skies and bare trees rattling in sharp winds. Only the diner coffee is hot. And the fireplace in Odysseia's suite.

Odysseia is only in Illinois for 5 days, but the number of bags she brought is incongruous. It takes 2 bellboys 2 trips each to ferry them all to room 919. Armless Odysseia tips them with a $20 extended from between her toes. She asks one to start the fire and turn the bed covers: not the usual duties of bellboys, but then she isn't their usual guest. Jetlagged from the 9-hour flight, Odysseia wants only to sleep.

She awakes with a gasp some indeterminable amount of time later. The room is hot—far too hot. The gas fireplace still blazes and Odysseia and her bed are both soaked. She kicks the covers off and shimmies over the side of the bed, noting in a sleep-daze the bedside clock. 0100 hours. 1 AM. She sighs. She'd only meant to take a nap, and now she's screwed up her sleep schedule royally.

Odysseia walks to where her suitcases are still stacked by the door. She kicks the first one onto its side and unzips it with a foot. Flipping back its flap, she finds the packable potters' wheel, the small collapsible stool; sets them up and plugs the electric wheel into a converter then into the wall. She opens the door and checks the hallway: yes, the clay she asked for at the front desk has been delivered. It waits innocently in a rolled brown paper sack. Heavy, she scoots the package into the room with her instep. Keeps inching it toward its new resting place by the fire.

MONICA is in Chicago wrapping up a 6-week trial for an out-of-state client when she sees the bus stop banner advertising Odysseia's exhibit in the capitol city. She changes her flight to leave two days later from Springfield, and catches the Amtrak south instead of the blue line to O'Hare. The train gets into Springfield at midnight. Monica claims her usual suite at the Otterwood Hotel. She's fumbling with her keycard when the damp and disheveled face of Odysseia pokes out from a door down the hall. Monica watches Odysseia pull a paper bag into her room with one leg. Odysseia doesn't notice Monica. Monica, silenced by shock, doesn't say a word.

Back in 919, Odysseia plunks a clay ball onto her wheel. She's disrobed entirely, unable to open the room's safety-glass windows for airflow, and unwilling to dim the fire's flickering light.

On Saturday the tiny door is a slide, and tumbling from its exit in a towheaded heap comes a three-year-old **LORRIE**, soft and full of joy. She slumps over to one side and giggles, the sound as light and warm as her baby-white hair, curly yet around the ears and with a pleasant bulge at her thighs that all that toddling hasn't managed to melt away. Though little Lorrie hasn't said a word—only smiled and laughed open-mouthed, revealing milk teeth—32-year-old Lorrie knows the little girl is her own younger self.

Gingerly, she approaches, sits down on the floor next to her dæmon, and wraps her in a hug that feels like arms wrapping around Lorrie. She sighs and feels the rightness of it all. The purity of a touch that is love sent through time to and from the child she was. A reminder that they (she) has made it, and there is much to be thankful for and much to embrace in the right now. Namely that everything is okay, and Lorrie never was and never will be alone.

Wrapped in Lorrie's hug, Little Lorrie makes a half-hearted struggle. She's trying to indicate that she wants to stand. Lorrie scoots back to give Lor-Lor room, but immediately recognizes the problem. Little Lorrie has no toes. All ten have been cut off and scarred over in knobby little mounds, making balance difficult and walking near impossible. Lorrie feels a corresponding twinge in her own pinky toe—the one she cut off accidentally, and the one they sewed back asymmetrically. Her toe looks gray in the still-dark dawn-lit room, and then she realizes it's a dirt smear. She swabs at her toe with a licked finger. Absorbed, she momentarily forgets about Lor-Lor.

When Lorrie next looks at her younger self, she wonders if the painkillers that Bartholomew had prescribed post-tonsillectomy are finally kicking in. Lor-Lor lies motionless on a toy box in the middle of the room, directly beneath the guillotine that's drawn Lorrie's dreams for weeks now. The girl doesn't look scared but the blade looks sharp. It falls as Lorrie sprints the ten feet that separate them, throwing the full weight of protection, of adult agency, on the tender soul who has none.

Two doors down, **MONICA** argues with herself. Does she knock on the artist's door or let the giant, slobbering, sleeping dog lie? The two women hadn't parted in Copenhagen on bad terms necessarily—but sex and words unspoken both carry a gravity that demands to be addressed or is doomed to haunt the heart, rules be damned. Monica thinks back to the moment of goodbye. She'd gifted Odysseia a fox tooth from the totems at her throat and Odysseia had smiled sadly. "I'll use it in my next sculpture," she'd said, but she hadn't kissed Monica goodbye. It is the non-kiss that throws Monica off now. It is the prospect of claiming that kiss that makes her don the hotel's terrycloth robe and slippers and pad to room 919.

Suddenly bashful, Monica puts her ear to the door and listens. She hears nothing inside; maybe Odysseia has gone to bed. What would a fox do? Bat her long eyelashes and curl up with her mate in the den. Monica knocks.

A white noise *whirring* that Monica only notices in its absence goes silent behind the door.

"Who is it?" Odysseia calls.

"Monica," Monica whispers, knowing she isn't loud enough but unable to access her confident courtroom voice.

"Hello?" Odysseia calls again.

"It's Monica," the sometimes-shaman says more loudly. "Can I come in?"

There is a second of quiet consideration, then Odysseia kicks her key card beneath the door and into the hallway. It is easier for room service and visitors to let themselves in than for Odysseia to answer the door with one foot.

Monica taps the plastic card to the magnetic pad and the lock clicks open effortlessly. She edges the door inward a crack. "Odysseia?"

The whirring has started up again.

Monica pushes the door open and goes in.

The first thing she notices is the intense heat. It's like walking into a wall of superheated jello: liquid and solid and instantly worming itself into underarm crevice and hip crease. Perspiration beads like shower steam. Next she notices the flickering firelight. It throws shadows big as monsters or a whole harem of ladies of the night across the bed's comforter and leaning into the corners of the room. Only once Monica's eyes adjust can she make out Odysseia seated before a small spinning pottery wheel. The artist is completely naked. As Odysseia forms a small vase with her feet from a mound of dripping clay, her full womanhood is on display. Monica feels her pulse leap with the flames.

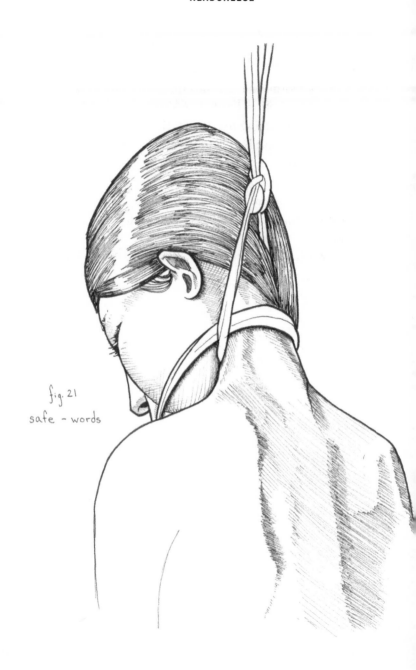

fig. 21
safe - words

The after-sex cigarette. It's a stereotype made popular by good-looking actors, their fuzzy chests pillowed beneath the spilling hair of sated leading ladies. That cigarette—it says something about completion: about an act attempted and the pride of the man who believes (perhaps correctly) that he has done well. God looked at the world he had created and pronounced it good. Saw that men and women fit together in a way that both would miss in the other's absence. Man wasn't made for cold dinners alone, just as housewives don't set their hair because it makes them happy. We're playing roles.

After the operation, **GEORGE** sits at the dinner table smoking. Heat mirages shimmer in the air outside his window, made softer by long, slow exhales of remnant tobacco. The sides of his head are warm. Sticky. Red. Patched with a fox tooth and an eagle talon. The spam on his plate is sticky and redly warm.

He taps ash into **SARAH**'s ring dish.

MONICA finally comes to George in his sleep. "You're late," he says, but not accusatorially. Instead he observes how she never did open her door. "I needed you," he admits, more willing to be vulnerable now, more confessional than everyday elder prudence dictates. Monica smiles at him, nonverbal; but something in her smile is sad and George has time to notice that Monica looks a little purple. Maybe she stands waving from beneath an ultraviolet light or maybe it's what she looks like when she becomes Nihimá, Great Mother—but the purple makes her white eyes and her white lawyer teeth gleam yellow and animalian and George can't figure out whether this animal is predator or prey. Whether she can help him, or will in fact watch him devour himself.

Ol' One-Arm is back at volleyball tonight. I decide I can't really feel sorry for him because he almost never misses a return. Even if his flail doesn't make the ball arc perfectly to the setter's waiting hands, the athlete keeps it air-bound. And hey—they win. It goes to three games but still they win and I can't help but notice his 6'2" height and broad chest. Once I dive face-first for a dig and mouth open take a gobful of crunchy sand. Sitting up and spitting, I am overcome by the urge to drag my sandpaper tongue all over his scarred shoulder stump (how scarred and what colors I can only imagine) but the sweat-salty taste of skin over muscle.

I want him until I notice the earring: a cubic zirconium stud. Then I don't want him anymore.

Tomorrow I will go to the grocery store and buy a veal shoulder and put it in the crockpot and wait for the meat to cook and the smell of au jus to fill the kitchen (such a homey, comforting, mouth-watering smell). I will lift the lid and run a hungry tongue along the shoulder and I will wonder if writing this book is giving me an amputee fetish. Unless subconsciously it was already there.

DON knows the best way to keep a secret is to let as many people as possible know just enough about the situation to keep up appearances and keep out inquiring noses. So he goes straight to **CARLOS**'s keeper (his mama) and explains how he wishes to hire Carlos for some jobs on his property and would that be okay with Mrs. Delgada? Surely she'd enjoy the couple extra hours/day that Don'd take the man-child off of her hands, and Mrs. Delgada thinks it a fine deal indeed, what with the extra physical exertion sure to tucker her boy out, make him sleep better at night, fewer night terrors and whatnot. And with the extra money it'd be like Carlos was after all these years finally contributing to the family. So Mrs. Delgada beams and waves as Don drives off with Carlos sitting in the bed of his truck, and that is the beginning of Day 1.

On Day 1, Don teaches Carlos to work the manual transmission in his mud truck: an '83 beater that often chokes on its own blue emissions but serves just fine to haul equipment around the farm. Because Carlos doesn't speak, Don asks him to nod if he understands the short speech about gears and clutches. Carlos does nod so to test him Don sends Carlos to the barn on the back forty to pick up some rakes, saying if Carlos isn't back in fifteen minutes, Don will come after him in the Gator. Carlos gets back in the truck's dusty driver's seat and with a horrible grating sound manages to force the shifter from neutral to first and then he is off, the truck irregularly coughing blue smoke and jerking with ill-timed gear changes.

On Day 1, Carlos makes it back with two rakes in fifteen minutes and side-by-side in silence the two men rake clean for two more hours the path that leads from Don's back door to the ridge at the far end of his property line. At 6 PM, Don drives Carlos home. Carlos sits in the back of the truck bed. Don pays his new worker and sends him in for dinner, then goes home for dinner himself. Followed by a snifter of scotch and a slice and a half of **PETUNIA**'s world-famous pie. In his bed later, Carlos masturbates, and in their bed later, Don makes love to his wife for the first time in three months.

Thereafter, on Mondays they mow. On Tuesdays they rake and mulch and weed. On Wednesdays they move the irrigation hoses and on Thursdays they collect kindling and pillage the orchard for ripe fruits to take to Petunia. On Fridays, beautiful Fridays, Don mucks the horse stalls while Carlos chops wood and then they spend the last thirty minutes stacking the split logs neatly in the last stall. There are only a couple horses, so Don always takes his time, pausing often and under the pretense of sprinkling fresh straw to sweep around more microscopic dust while secretly staring at Carlos. *Whack. Thwack.* The boy is a machine. Every log splits evenly every time. He never misses his mark and his work is quick as it is clean. Don lavishes the boy with profuse praise, man-to-man encouragement, and long, rambling unselfconscious soliloquies about Renaissance art of all things—Leonardo and the perfection of the human form. Carlos never disagrees or interrupts or even acknowledges his boss for that matter beyond the occasional nod. Don permits himself to imagine that Carlos would if he only could second everything that Don says.

Then again, the boy is slow all right. When he'd had Carlos sign a work contract and liability waiver, the seventeen-year-old had scrawled what may not in court even pass for an X. And Don had smiled.

LORRIE's throat hurts too badly in the days following the surgery for her to want anything other than a popsicle or ice chips near her mouth. She doesn't even want to kiss **BARTHOLOMEW** and he is anyway repulsed by her blood-sweet breath. For three nights in a row he goes down on her for hours, expecting nothing in return. While the moans she can't stifle scrape up from her diaphragm passed her clotted throat, the pain is nothing compared to the pleasure he gives her. Had given her on stage. Will give to her again.

On Thursday Lorrie wakes with a start. She'd dreamed of the girl again, and the guillotine. Where before that quivering blade had always promised release, she doesn't like that now it is the girl on the table. Her three-year-old self. Helpless and scared and unlike Lorrie wanting to be anywhere but there.

Lorrie hears the clink of ceramic mug on counter in the kitchen and calls to Bartholomew.

Making love to **VICKI** is completely different than fucking the First Lady in a broom closet. Where the latter was coarse and exciting and made him feel powerful—as though, for a moment, he was the president of the United States, and not just some robotics grunt with top-secret security clearance—the former—his Vicki—the sweet, soft (infinitely soft) Vicki—is slow and intentional and it bothers him not a whit that she holds all the power. **TRICE** wants her to have it, to own it. To relax and be happy after eighteen unimaginable years raising a child on her own. His child. **FOREST**.

Their reconciliation doesn't happen overnight. We don't cut from the hospital scene—one grieving parent and one befuddled parent staring helplessly at the mutilated body of their son—to a shot of the happily-reunited couple moving against one another in bed. There are eighteen years to make up for, to reconcile in the checkbook, and to understand where they can possibly go from here. She's pretty as ever, if not worry-hardened. He's suddenly out of his element, ripped from the stable life he'd built and at a loss for how to say, "I'm sorry, Vicki. I wish I'd known." The most straightforward, honest words never seem like enough.

He starts showing up at her apartment to cook her dinner. Sometimes she lets him hold her hand under the table, and they don't say much. Vicki nibbles at Trice's bachelor notions of 'meals,' and then one night she asks if he's seen a popular movie. "It's on Netflix," she offers. When he says "No, but I'd like to" they watch the movie, and that night they fall asleep on the couch. When Vicki wakes up cold at 4 AM she snuggles into the man who has changed in most ways but not the important ones. His arms wrap protectively, unconsciously, around her.

The night they take things one step farther—one step

closer to each other—it's Forest's birthday. Trice has decided to present Forest with the new prosthesis at dinner, before the boy goes out with his friends. Vicki offers to cook and Forest asks if he can invite a friend, and with a meaningful look at Trice, Vicki says yes. When the doorbell rings at seven, they're expecting a girl.

But it's **CARLOS**. Tall, slow, carelessly handsome Carlos. Trice steps out of the way to let him inside and Vicki is extending her hand, smiling, relieved that Forest isn't growing up too fast after all. Until the niggling doubt—could it still be a date? Could Forest be gay? But although Carlos accepts her handshake, he offers no verbal clues to confirm or deny his intentions—his orientation—and then Forest is hugging his friend. "Carlos!" He slaps the man-child's back enthusiastically. "You made it, man!" Carlos, pleased, smiles, and that's when Trice and Vicki see the sloppy grin, the black half-teeth, and realize just who Carlos must be. A 'friend,' all right. From work! Trice and Vicki are unaware that their shoulders collectively sag back into normalcy from somewhere up around their ears.

Everyone enjoys dinner. Forest had requested enchiladas, and they're gooey with onions and cheese. They make mouths stick together, somewhat impeding conversation, somewhat alleviating the awkward fact that Carlos would have little to contribute anyway. After dinner there is ice cream and after ice cream there are three gifts for Forest to open. A smart button-down shirt from Mom. A candy bar from Carlos's pocket, half-melted. A new arm.

Trice is gratified to see Forest's eyes light up at the lightweight prosthesis. He handles the arm with his one left arm, turning it this way and that in admiration. Forest notices the bluetooth fibers. "Can it—" Trice cuts him off before he can finish, warming up now to his favorite topic. "Yeah. It's practically mind-controlled," he enthuses. "The limb responds within microseconds of you thinking a motion—almost precognitively. Of course—" but Forest is already hugging him, crushing the titanium arm between their bodies. Except who's kidding? Nothing can crush that baby, ever more indestructible than an arm of flesh and bone.

Then Carlos walks home and Forest goes out and Vicki is so grateful for Trice's gift to Forest that she offers herself to him. In that way they find each other again, across the years and in between what was and what will be.

My greatest fear is becoming paralyzed. Paralysis means becoming dependent. Dependence means it's harder to run away. You have to stay and face the music. No mercy. No control; utterly at the whim of someone else. Stuck in a chair in a bed in a sling, someone emptying my bed pan. Rolling me over to dress my bedsores. Unable to look away from whatever nameless horizon. My greatest fear is becoming paralyzed.

But your greatest fear might be staying stuck in a body you never wanted. Could never identify with. A pathology known as dysmorphia. Addressed in the news last week as transableism. Not transgender but wishing to transform from able-bodied to disabled and ashamed to let anyone know the truth.

One man has an accident with a power saw. He doesn't plan it. He hadn't learned in advance how to stop the bleeding. (He did and he had.)

One woman wears leg braces because she needs them. She spends most of her time in a wheelchair, unable to otherwise locomote comfortably. (Not.)

Another man innocently fails his hearing test. His eye test. His driver's test. He is prescribed and fitted for adaptive.corrective.prosthetic devices. (He makes these choices intentionally.)

Disability.

Dis. Ability.

Dis. Ability.

Dis. Abil.	Ity.		
Dis. A.	Bil.	Ity.	
Dis. A.	Bil.	I.	Ty.

Disabil. Ity.

Decibel. Ity.

Decibility.

More than 65 decibels of hearing loss is considered legally deaf.

GEORGE leaves the satellite dishes of his ears in the trash without a backward glance. They keep focusing the signal like a honing mechanism. Like a homing device. Without them, he is finally blessedly free. No more will the dead haunt his head with their incessant demands to be heard even in death. It's pitiful, really—the vain attempt to atone for a life unlived from beyond the grave. George laughs. His own voice sounds far away. Curdled.

Imagine seeing someone you don't know on the street. They're clearly hurt and just as clearly oblivious to the blood. Do you approach (cautiously)? Ask if they're okay? Offer a hanky hand-embroidered by your great-grand-mother? Do you stare awkwardly and hope someone else is up to the task?

On Monday, the first student to see George knows the old man by reputation only. It's George Maa'itsoh. An elder and a legend, even if slightly more decrepit in his advancing age. The student named **WEEKO** decides that George looks unwell. Confused. There are blood stains at his collar. Blood seems to be leaking from the flaps of his beaver fur cap.

Weeko falls in stride with George. "Azhé'é (our father)," she addresses him. "Are you okay? I think you're bleeding." George doesn't reply. Acts in fact as if she isn't there. He keeps walking. He doesn't hear her.

That night, Weeko meets a boy at a bar. An Asian boy from New York, in Arizona on business and drowning his sorrows at the casino where Weeko works. Weeko can tell that **IRA** is hurt, too, though it's his heart and not his head that's bleeding. She sees the tight, tailored pants, the fine leather shoes, the pout in his lower lip, and thinks *Gay*. She serves him five Hendricks. Later, she is surprised to find Ira waiting for her in the parking lot when she finishes her shift.

"Let's go," he says, puddling off the roof of his car and opening her door. That night, Weeko learns how to choke a cock. (Funny, she'd thought you could only choke on them.) She holds Ira when, afterward, he cries.

On **FOREST**'s nineteenth birthday, he kisses **VICKI**'s cheek and thanks her for the enchiladas. He shakes his father's (it still feels weird to think that word) hand and thanks him for the arm. He fits it to his shoulder like the pimped-out status symbol it is, and heads to his favorite D.C. club: the one where the bouncers always look the other way. Yeah, the kid's nineteen. And he fuckin' lost his fuckin' arm in a war nobody believes in. He's cool.

On Forest's nineteenth birthday, he fist-bumps **UMI** the bouncer with his slick-as-shit new ice machine and the party lights glance off the shiny alloy. The reflection catches the attention of **ANNA** across the floor. It seems to wink at her: an invitation. With glow stick bracelets stacked like scars at her wrists, she goes over to investigate.

Every chalice has its own miniature altar: a raised, co-lumnar pedestal with a plexiglass cage on top that simul-taneously protects the artworks and affords a 360-degree view of their intricate details. Fashioned by foot from Moroccan clay, embedded with human and animal teeth, small stones fastidiously mosaic-ed, **ODYSSEIA**'s latest exhibit is astonishing. All the more so for the story be-hind it—so **LORRIE** takes museum patrons behind-the-scenes and for once she doesn't mind the spotlight.

The camera crew is filming a mini-documentary. A *Sixty Minutes*-type[78] story for local television. Lorrie starts by showing off the crates that Odysseia's pieces were packed in for shipping. "It looks like a suitcase," the anchor points out, and Lorrie agrees. "Yep, that's for easy handling. The lightweight hard shell is reaction injection molded polyurethane, the same material cases for musical instruments are made out of." Lorrie pops the catch and opens the suitcase. "The interior is lined with foam core that then 'floats' the cavity-packed artifact or art object. Each chalice is cradled immovably."

"Did the museum build these?"

Lorrie gestures to the two engineers watching from the corner. "Yes, we're very proud to have a top-notch exhibits team who not only builds the crates to ship ar-tifacts safely, but creates such beautiful displays as well." She waves at the chalice pedestals.

"Why chalices?" the anchor prompts.

"Let's ask the artist, shall we?"

The camera swings over to Odysseia. "Mrs. Baines—"

"*Miss* Baines. Odysseia," she corrects them.

"Miss Baines, you heard the question. What can you tell us about the chalices?"

---

[78] An American newsmagazine television program broadcast on the CBS television network.

"My chalices are modeled after the ones that a small group of northern-sympathizing Jesuit priests used to administer communion to Union troops during the Civil War," Odysseia explains. "These blessed men would offer the blood of that divine young man called Jesus in chalices to civilian soldiers. So there's a lot of masculine energy wrapped up in what has traditionally been a symbol of the feminine." As Lorrie watches the artist speak, she finds herself wondering: had Odysseia been the type to talk with her hands when she had them?

"Obviously, the Roman Catholic Church is a patriarchy. But if you go back far enough, to the pagan roots of the church, you find a very different connotation of the chalice as a metaphor for a woman's womb. The bowl of the uterus, like a half-full cup, fills up with the blood of new life. The goddess figure is actually more powerful than the church that subverted her, because when woman is inverted (as in some sex acts), the contents of her cup don't runneth over. She is always receiving and forever a safe harbor for anyone who comes to her in need."

"Are those brass buttons on the cups? And…teeth? Are those teeth?"

"Yes, but they're all replicas. I've used real artifacts in other series, but given that this exhibit was commissioned by a museum whose mission it is to preserve Civil War memorabilia, I thought it prudent to respect their policies. So I poured the buttons in molds at my workshop, and the teeth are ceramic. Maybe there's a vagina dentata message there, or maybe I'm just extra grateful for my teeth now that I don't have claws."

Odysseia smiles and Lorrie does, too.

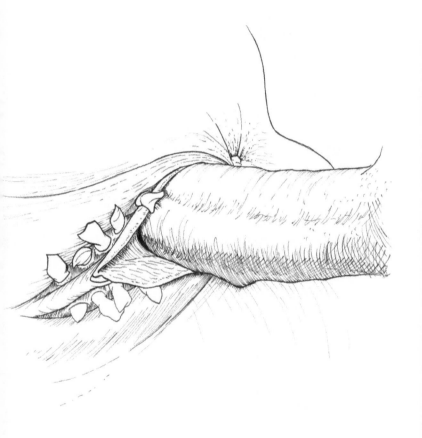

In the background of the shot, a group of men, several of them amputees, can be seen approaching the exhibit.

"And what is the message to veterans here?" the anchor asks.

"War is violence unsanctified," Odysseia begins. "Which is to say: violence committed in the name of destroying an enemy. The blood of the chalice, on the other hand, is the fruit of constructive violence. Blood shed in the name of purgation, of creation—the way that women are no less whole but lighter, freer, after a week of menstruation."

Don leads the support group closer to hear what Odysseia is saying. Through the eye of the camera, he appears to stop directly behind her.

"The message to veterans, especially those suffering from PTSD, is that restoration and healing are possible."

On camera, the bodies of the artist with no arms and the man with one leg align. For a moment, Odysseia has arms again, and Don—two whole legs. Then he shifts his weight and the illusion is broken.

"You're from Copenhagen," the anchor is saying. "Why the American Civil War?"

"It's a good question," Odysseia admits. "Frankly, I believe I am the Civil War surgeon Dr. Horace C. Braker reincarnated." Off-screen, Lorrie's jaw drops open in disbelief. "My mission in every lifetime is to help the wounded heal."

ELIOT starts, as all responsible citizens in this day and age must, with copious internet research. The images are too graphic at first and he wonders, *If they make my stomach turn, how can it also be what I want?* Disgust is perennially at odds with desire. But he can't shake the memory of how he felt that night in Springfield, or the conversation that followed back at Lorrie and **BARTHOLOMEW**'s apartment. Lorrie, of course, hadn't contributed much. She'd gargled with salt water and gone to bed. Bartholomew and Eliot had stayed up swallowing scotch at the kitchen table, where Eliot had talked and Bartholomew had listened. By the time Eliot had stumbled toward Lorrie's thrift store sedan, the two men had hatched a plan.

But back in New York, the plan feels less plausible and more like the ramblings of two drunks: one confused, and one quite possibly deranged. Who in their right mind amputated anyone who asked? Who in their right mind wanted to be amputated?

Over a cup of corner deli soup and a beer (in his depression over losing Ira, El had manifested the beginnings of a belly) Eliot stared at his phone, willing it for the thousandth time to ring. For Ira's name to appear in white type and for Ira to plead with unusual contriteness, *Please, baby. Come home.* But it never does and chances are that Ira has long forgotten Eliot, and that El prays fervently.uselessly.idiotically to the void.

The void.

Eliot navigates back to the browser tab still open on his screen. He's seen a million different penises in a million different porn videos, but none of them looked like this.

On Friday, the link goes live on the internet. It is closely tracked to monitor how and to whom it spreads. With every missive, Church gains more followers. **CAPTAIN HOOK** announces that the flock is growing, and that the bystander effect will not be tolerated. You participate or you are exiled. Because voyeurism is a legitimate form of participation, all it takes is showing up when Church comes to your city. "We worship in the temples of the reviled," Captain Hook adds to New York's invitation. "Our blood sacrifices please no god but ourselves." For good measure, there's a textbook-grade photo of Lorrie's flayed left tonsil pinned next to a ruler and a standard offset color bar.

GEORGE walks until he finds the coyotes. They've been waiting for him.

Delirious with dehydration and infection (his ear no longer rings but 'pop' occasionally as another pus-filled sun blister bursts), he believes he walks toward **SARAH**. He can't see her, but sometimes he thinks he hears her, her kind laughter rising on the wind like a howl. On Thursday, he collapses at noon in the desert, miles from civilization. On Thursday, Sarah finds him at sundown. Her hair brushes his face like a tail. As each coyote grabs a different limb and pulls, George looks like a starfish from above. His arms and legs twisting apart. His gold canine eyes staring at nothing.

"I was born with a congenital anomaly called sym-brachydactyly," **ODYSESSIA** answers the anchor matter-of-factly. "I had no left arm at all, and my right was dwarfed, a foreshortened lump of fingerlets attached bonelessly to my elbow. It was ugly and used to scare the other children, the way it just dangled there uselessly. Whenever I got excited and flapped my arm, it clapped against my side body like an obese woman's batwing. No bones, no tendons, no structure at all. A skin sac. On my nineteenth birthday, I had my body correction."

"Do you mean you had your arm medically amputated?"

"I mean I had my arm amputated by the seamstress in my hometown."

The anchor doesn't know what to say.

"Ribe is a very small town. The barber doubled as the doctor. While his blade was sharp, his accuracy was somewhat dulled by his whiskey habit. The seamstress's scissors were just as sharp, and she never drank."

"Scissors."

"Oh, yes. It was like cutting through a boneless chicken breast. And her stitch job was the neatest I've ever seen. Hardly a scar."

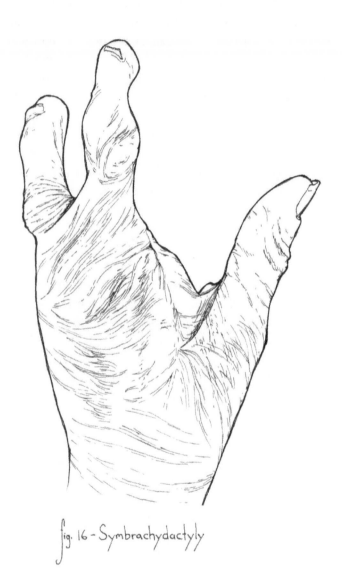

fig. 16 - Symbrachydactyly

On Saturday, **IRA** watches the burning of the Zozobra on the Navajo reservation. His confession is lost somewhere among the countless slips of paper about to catch fire inside the doll's papier-mâché body. Once it burns, Ira's secret will die with it. This small token of apology, however ephemeral, is all he can manage at the moment. "Dear El," the note reads. "I'm a fucking soulless robot. I'm sorry I couldn't love you."

ANNA likes the way her smooth caramel skin looks against **FOREST**'s chocolate milk complexion. She is the product of two different unions: sperm to egg, and hand to wrist. Forest is, too; only his donor limb was grown in a lab rather than in or on the body of another. Together, they represent some third, alien being: a cyborg hellbent on proving that robots really can love.

Ad for an amputated limb, for sale on eBay:

One right lower leg and foot. Leg unshaved. Fine hair the color of dirty airport carpet. Hair is approximately .5" long. Skin color: rain-soggy earthworm (or tanned peach). Toes: 5. Currently painted Island Breeze (bright teal). Please advise if you would like toe nails to be polished a different color in advance of mailing, have the lacquer removed, or sent as-is. Grade B tan lines where sandal straps (size 9) rested in summer. Lateral suture scars around circumference of pinky toe (previously cut off in an accident and erroneously reattached, as subject was still a minor). Calluses at anterior big toe from shoes; a slightly cracked heel from running in the rain. No discernible birthmarks or other pronounced pigmentations. No tattoos. Moldable, buffable, for fetish play. Available for castings. Seller will divide upon request.

Homeless smells just a bit different in Chicago. As if there's sea salt mixed in. Which doesn't really make any sense, since Lake Michigan only wants to be the ocean with its summertime imported palm trees. The salt makes Chicago flesh earthier somehow. Not so sharp on the nostrils—though the unwashed themselves must work that much harder to get your attention, to make up for it. "You are less likely to smell my smell," they are saying, "so I will jerk around extra wildly in my seat and rub my nylon windbreaker compulsively because I like the sound it makes, like the wind at night—and I'll start scratching myself so hard in one thick-skinned spot that I'll make you think you have lice.fleas.mites, too. Haha. I think it's funny."

Signs on Chicago's elevated train say that continuous riding is not allowed, but they ride the L all night anyway. Bent over backpacks containing all their worldly posses-sions. Raising heads at announced stops to mutter "Shit" and go back to sleep. Until this year.

Last year the trendy dare was to light a homeless person on fire. Walk up to where he's sleeping in the concrete doorway of some foreign retailer's stoop, shake the dregs from Daddy's can of gasoline, strike and throw the match. It made the news but didn't make so good a story, skedaddling soon as the cotton caught, leaving no evidence other than an eyewitness 'friend' to prove it was you who done the deed.

No, this year it's amputation. Young bodies pin a man's body to the floor of the train, stretching out an arm, forcing the palm flat to the tile. Sometimes a switchblade handy for the purpose, and sometimes little better than a dull kitchen knife. It's always better if the man is Hispanic. Short un mano the next day, the boys will saunter by him again, already out of the hospital, and if bold, brave, or apathetic, back in his usual seat on the L.

"Yo, man. Let's hang. Mano a mano, no?" The joke cracks them up every time.

TRICE hesitates to become a real part of **FOREST**'s life. He watches him from the sidelines, silently cheering every time his son swishes in some pick-up basketball game in one of D.C.'s many urban parks. Just another young black man. Athletic. Good-looking. Dusk glinting off the sweat on his forehead; the screws in his prosthetic arm.

In 1954, in Small Town, Kansas, high school let out earlier in the day than middle school, so young men could get home to help their fathers on the farm. T. was 14 and a freshman the afternoon his right arm got sucked into a piece of farm machinery. It separated below the elbow with a wet *thwuck* and was spit out somewhere on the field below, bloody and never for a moment looking real. T.'s younger sisters were called from their shared classroom (it housed the 5th through 8th grades) and told to report to the hospital immediately.

T. had to relearn how to write—this time with his left hand. How to pull a trigger. Pitch a hay fork. Rub one out in the mornings. He discovered he hated his sisters' perfect arms, so intact and pale from doing only house-work. Weak arms. Useless on women. Men needed their arms to work. Men needed arms, period.

What a man doesn't need is his nose. What a man deserves to lose when he cuts the nose-horn off a rhino is his own nose. A hooked fillet knife tracing and delicately peeling the nose skin of poachers from their faces. Blood spills from black faces bright as a bawling black rhino's. Both muscled beasts reduced to infants, frightened and calling for their mothers.

On Sunday, **LORRIE** doesn't have to pinch herself to know that she's not dreaming. The guillotine is real. She watched her lover build it in the spare bedroom.

The device looks like any other desktop paper cutter. Heavy metal base. Free-swinging arm. Blade shiny as **BARTHOLOMEW**'s furrowed forehead.

He loves the idea; he doesn't love the mess: a limb. A piece left behind. Blood to catch by the bucketful. It just isn't the clean aesthetic he normally gravitates toward. And yet the cut this particular tool calls for will be cleaner than any cut even the sharpest longsword could deliver.

Bartholomew lifts the weighted arm, settling it gently into a metal catch. He leans over. Purses his lips, and makes as if to kiss the blade. The slightest pressure change from his exhalation causes the arm to release. It drops without whisper or shudder, finding the mark of its rubberized cradle, and freezing still as death—like it had never moved at all.

Satisfied, Captain Hook drapes the cutter with a cloth,

and wheels the steel table backstage.

J. made us watch *American Mary*[79] a couple nights ago. I don't know what the title is a reference to except maybe *American Psycho*[80]—but that was all in his head, and this was definitely real because the characters died too creatively. The only thing to do when your professor rapes you is to start amputating his limbs. You have six hours from the time an arm is cut off to reattach it.

Or else tissue necrosis.

Today a woman boarded the bus carrying a styrofoam cooler and my only thought was 'organs.' I felt like it should have the word on a fancy red sticker, or at the very least, written in Sharpie, because maybe I made the whole thing up and it was only a beer, or a half-eaten baloney sandwich.

---

[79] A 2012 Canadian horror film.

[80] A 1991 novel by Bret Easton Ellis, adapted for the screen in 2000.

A homeless man, anonymous, but also named Jeff, had to have part of his foot amputated. He's another smart schizophrenic. He walks around on that half-stump, and the wound never heals. It just becomes bigger. It's only a little bit infected. Jeffrey's legs are as fat and spotted as the offspring of a hippo and a giraffe. Do we know for a fact that interspecies breeding is impossible? Or is it only because a giraffe has not yet fallen in love with a hippo?

NATANJALI's son grows up in a town renamed for his mother and henceforth known as the land of the women with breasts. He is proud of her legacy and while sad that he was too young at the time of his parents' deaths to remember them, nor can he really miss them. His grandfather and his cousin tell stories and cry sometimes around the fire in the evening, but as far as Natanjali's son is concerned, these two are his whole family—and he is happy.

At four years old, the beta is a fearless and high-spirited child. He gives his cousin heart attacks when he shows up for lunch with a monkey on his shoulders—rhesus macaques that are known for their aggressive temperaments and which hiss at P. until she throws a half-rotten fruit from the sill into the jungle, sending the monkey chasing after it, and leaving Natanjali's son stamping his bare brown foot. It's the tigers that P. is always warning him about, and the snakes, no matter that animals of every disposition from stray dogs to scorpions inordinately flock to the beta, the angels of their better natures leaving him unharmed.

One day, Natanjali's son sees a snake charmer in the market. While P.'s back is turned, poring over tins of dry tea, the beta approaches the young man and his swaying cobra. Watches the man's lithe fingers move nimbly over the hewn holes of a bone pipe. It would seem the snake charmer has also hypnotized himself. His eyes are closed, lost in the minor-key melody. He doesn't see the beta step far too close to the woven basket. Can't slap the boy's hand away as Natanjali's son reaches to pet the snake.

Although the music continues, with the beta's touch the spell is broken. The cobra regards him, hood flared, black eyes glinting curiously. It's possible that Natanjali's son, like his mother, is meant to leave his mark on the world. That, blessed by his mother's blood sacrifice, he has found special favor with the gods. Ganesha, the elephant god. Hanuman the monkey. Shesha, the great snake prince. Perhaps Natanjali's son is destined for amazing feats: displays of sensitivity and acts of compassion that will bridge the human-animal divide.

But a woman in the crowd, seeing the snake appear to size up the boy, screams. A circle opens up around the snake charmer, his basket, and the boy. The charmer, aware that sudden movements can startle wild animals, reaches slowly—very slowly—for the basket lid. The woman who screamed, feeling a sense of responsibility now, rushes quickly—very quickly—to the beta's side. She jerks him roughly away from the snake.

In the swirl of her sari skirts, no one sees the cobra, scared, strike.

P., suddenly realizing that her tiny cousin is at the heart of the commotion, pushes through to grab the beta's hand and pulls a disappearing act back into the shopping.staring.shouting throngs.

She doesn't ask if Natanjali's son is okay because she didn't see a thing. The beta looks down once at the two tiny holes in his pant leg. Sees the blood that is starting to stain. He doesn't say a word, knowing how upset his overprotective chachera bhaee would be.

Later, back at the house, he takes off his pants and he buries them in the deep mud by the river.

The snake charmer tries not to worry about his liability. Having removed the cobra's venom sacs himself, he feels confident that the child, had he been bitten, will be fine. At 19, however, he's forgotten how a child thinks. A child's tendency to guard secrets like treasure—whether the baby bunnies in the box under his bed, or the bite that three days later has swollen to a hard, red, enflamed thing—itchy like mad but too painful to scratch. Eventually too painful to walk on.

On Tuesday, P. tells Natanjali's son to get his butt to school if he doesn't want to be late. She assumes he's being cute, and then difficult, when he insists on scooting around on his behind instead of walking like a well-behaved child. Because the beta is small yet for his age, P. reaches for one extended foot, intending to string him up upside-down and deliver a proper wollop. When she grabs the boy's right ankle, low on the calf, he shrieks like he's been burned—and indeed P. can feel the heat through the boy's pants. She struggles to shimmy the beta's pant leg up, so large is the limb with infection. Helpless tears stream from the sorry eyes of Natanjali's son. P. scoops him up, runs him around the back of the house, and settles him in the basin, where she upends a whole bucket of cool river water onto his leg. The water doesn't steam though it might as well, given how hot the beta's leg is and how little the water's coolness does to soothe him.

Ayurvedic medicine can do nothing now. The damage is done. A team of American doctors on a mission to Cherthala determine that the only course of action is to amputate the beta's right leg before his cellulitis spreads further. Led by the experienced **DR. C.**, their decision is swift and the operation swifter. "But he's a boy! A little boy!" P. screams at the white coats as they wheel Natanjali's son away. "How will he play? He needs his leg to run and jump and play!" She sobs hysterically.

So that the beta may one day "run and jump and play" again, Dr. C. performs a Van Ness rotationplasty—whereby the still-viable foot is severed from the unsalvageable wreckage of calf, rotated 180 degrees, and re-attached backward at the knee joint, the ball of the heel becoming a crude kind of knee cap. It will allow Natanjali's son to more easily wear a prosthesis, and enjoy the mobility of a flexible joint.

What this well-meaning team of Western doctors doesn't understand is the way that superstition informs much of rural Indian culture. "Accidents" blamed on sorcery; deaths on witchcraft; calamities like snakebites on the will of wrathful gods. Did the little beta not do enough pujas? Fail to leave ample ladoos at the swami statue's feet?

And so the boy who would himself have become a swami became instead an outcast who lived off his family's charity until they died. An old man by then, he scooted through shit-filled streets on his behind and not even the sadhus shared their rice bowls, for being holy men themselves they would not associate with the earthbound demon with the backward foot ... the surest sign of a ghost or evil bhoot being backward-turned feet.

Natanjali's son fell from heaven's good grace and would return there no more.

UMI has always dreamed of being suspended. He dreamed of changing genders and having made that happen, believes now that anything is possible. When Church comes to DC, and Umi opens that black envelope, he contacts **CAPTAIN HOOK** to probe his areas of expertise. "I know next to nothing about suspension," Bartholomew says honestly. "But if you want, we can learn together."

When Captain Hook hoists Umi into the air, Umi remains completely still, as he has been taught. Limp and ragdoll-like, he swings inert and nearly lifeless, gone pale and sweaty with the pain; breath rapid and shallow with the thrill.

There will be scars, but no physical amputation. This is mental liberation. A cutting away of doubt. Reinterpreting possibility.

The building is abandoned now. Only the most intrepid of New York City's homeless constituency have dared take up residence there. Burnt walls black and smelling of soot when the wind blows just right. Dolls with half-faces, charred; Tonka trunks with their paint melted off. It used to be a daycare center, before the fire.

Tonight it's a Church, and all are welcome.

Homeless and affluent. Black and white. Men and women and those of no gender and at least one who has come to lose his sex. At the last minute, a wealthy stockbroker named **IRA** slips in the back.

The whole setting is more macabre than usual. Because the building hasn't had electricity for months, Bartholomew brings in generators. He arranges them around the main playroom's periphery, around piles of mounded ash. To the generators he connects what original fixtures are still in place. They consist of one hanging metal star lamp (its leaves die-cut and casting hundreds of pinpricks of light); a mobile heavy with flying dragons (their eyes and mouths glow red as the mobile turns, making the lullaby that accompanies their flight sound vaguely threatening); and a desk lamp salvaged from an adjacent office (its single incandescent bulb glares over a chair as though waiting to interrogate someone).

In the far back corner, two cribs hold two dusty bears like furry child corpses. Closer to the room's center is a playpen surrounded by scattered legos. These legos—they're the metaphor that Captain Hook wants center stage tonight. As varied in their colors, shapes, and sizes as the people in the room, they all serve one of two purposes: connection or stability. Main players or support staff. Some who will become a new creation, and some to bear witness. To say I see you; and to say Thy will be done. For as man has dominion over the earth and sky, so, too, does he over the holy vessel. The chalice. Or in this case, the sippy cup.

Captain Hook makes quick work of several wannabes seated in the spotlights cast by the star lamp. His bombs are getting better. Smaller and more directionally powerful with every iteration. Any more, the explosions barely make a sound. The simultaneous cytolysis of a billion cells at once is generally drowned out by the sigh of relief the initiates exhale—or if they're really lacking self-control, a low moan.

Bartholomew plugs their wounds with nipples from baby bottles. A discarded swaddling blanket and safety pins. Sets an accidentally dislocated ulna (jostled in the explosion) between the green roof slats from a Lincoln Logs box.

Church's congregation is always small and self-selecting. **ELIOT** is among their ranks; Captain Hook gestures to him. **LORRIE** squeezes Eliot's hand reassuringly, and then Captain Hook guides Eliot to the interrogation chair. Almost immediately, El grows hot beneath the bare bulb's blast.

Bartholomew produces a Bible. Eliot places his right hand upon it. "Do you swear to tell the truth—the whole truth—and nothing but the truth, so help you God?"

"I do."

"You may begin."

When Lorrie was 4, her bestest friend in the whole wide world was Jenni. Jenni lived next door and only the green snake of a garden hose, stretched long and capped by a lawn sprinkler, demarcated the line between her family's property and Lorrie's. Lorrie liked to go to Jenni's house because Jenni's parents often left the girls alone. Not that they ever got into too much trouble, but Lorrie struggled with authority from the beginning. In Jenni's empty house they watched *Annie*[81] on repeat and went through whole boxes of Ritz sandwich crackers, licking out only the processed cheese before sticking the two cracker discs back together, and back in the box.

On windy afternoons (of which there were many in that Midwestern tornado alleyway), Lorrie and Jenni would go outside to the garage. Lorrie would grab hold of the bottom edge of the garage door and Jenni would push the garage door button and up up up little Lor-Lor would rise, hanging and dangling and blowing in the breeze like a kite streamer from her automated lift. At the top, just before the door disappeared entirely into the blackness of the upper track, Lorrie would let go and drift down down down to the concrete driveway, the chalk designs that the girls had drawn the day before rushing back like a sun-faded memory.

Then it would be Jenni's turn to ride and Lorrie's turn to push the button. Jenni's turn to fly then fall, and Lorrie's turn to thrill with anticipation for her friend. If Jenni didn't let go in time, her fingers would be eaten by the unforgiving seam where door slid past door frame, retracting. They'd watched once as an unsuspecting caterpillar—the black- and orange-striped fuzzy-wuzzy kind—had not inched out of the way in time. As door

[81] A 1982 American musical comedy-drama film adapted from Broadway musical of the same name.

had scraped against door frame, the caterpillar had become a damp smear. Not orange and black, but green.

Having scraped her knee before, Lorrie knew that the inside of a girl was red; not green. *But boys*, she thought, *boys are probably green.*

And still there is something about the mashing that attracts her. A formerly living thing reduced to snot. A connected part—like a finger—separated. Amputated at the knuckle.

She watches **ELIOT** sweat under the spotlight. He's nervous, she knows. Never keen to be the one on display.

After Eliot finishes giving his statement: *Yes, this is what I want. I've thought about it for a long time. I haven't stopped thinking about it for a year.* Captain Hook guides him to the table—the one Lorrie's seen in all her dreams. The one she imagined Little Lor-Lor strapped to. But Eliot is not a victim.

As the blade drops, separating Eliot from a part of himself, **IRA**'s face in the back of the room goes green. Just before he vomits all the liquor that had given him the courage to show up in the first place—to think, however stupidly, that there was any chance at all for reconciliation—Lorrie gets her answer. Some boys, and some girls, too, are green. With jealousy. Or bilious with the toxic weight of words unsaid.

Armies used to sever the penises of the fallen as a way to count the dead.

A man used gardening shears to cut off his penis. He then flushed it down the toilet, all in the name of deterring a gay man who was stalking him. Both later appeared on Springer.

On Monday, four college-aged women meet at the coffeeshop for Bible study. Tonight they're looking at Colossians __, sharing what they 'appreciate' about the text. Dissecting passages and encouraging each other to keep the faith—to walk the path of the chaste and righteous. To be the keepers of their sisters- and brothers-in-Christ. It's kind of interesting and kind of sad. The light in their eyes is dimmed by the smugness of believing they're better than you.

You. With your dark Jew curls (though a Catholic). Eyes genuinely twinkling and so much more alive than those who in being born again, first had to die. The girls have zombie eyes. Makeup hides the pallor of their skin. But your cheeks have been pinched pink by the winter air. Your orthodontically-straightened teeth flash white as you say, "Come here, bella." As I nestle my head into your acne-pitted chest—yoga-strong and Italian—you start quoting JPII's Theology of the Body to me. And although it's religious—penned by a celibate white man; approved by the rich white Vatican—your voice; those words; they turn me on. Worshipping at the temple of your lover's body. You suction your mouth on my salt-lick skin and my temple walls are limestone. Granite. Marble. Built to withstand the wrecking ball of your gaze and make you proud.

Do you know how much I want you? All of you?

Want to eat you so that no one else can have you?

You're in Oregon now, slitting the bellies of river salmon with a knife handmade in Alaska. You scoop their insides out while the fish is still alive, forgoing bashing or cutting off their heads first. The head will be part of the final presentation. There are plastic bits and nails in a couple of their stomachs. That island of trash at the middle of the sea.

It doesn't even matter that it's trash. I'd still want to be marooned there with you.

Once the planet was a Pangaea—a supercontinent connected. The land stretched out its starfish arms and pulled.twisted.pulled itself apart into Africa and Antarctica, the Balkans and the Philippines. A body dismembered and some parts sinking into the depths: sediment. Fish food. Some parts bobbing like apples at Halloween: tiny islands. Still other parts spurting lava from severed arteries. Raw openings to the center of the earth. The core of the one hot thing. Seas boiling then cooling then global warming and a president who says it ain't real. We'll use fossil fuels because they're there and we're alive to use them, no matter it means sucking marrow from Hedwig's[82] milk-less teat. Let's drain the blood of the global body. Why not? Let's drill into.pull out the parts that like teeth appear optional—until we're left gumming our way through the stringy roast beef, unable to eat. Unable to fight back. Those canines though. Those dogteeth.

If you ever think of me, you never tell me. Maybe, like me, you write letters that go unsent, having consciously amputated communication. Maybe you just go home to your wife. Marriage amputating the possibility of the Other.

The young women? They're discussing 'animals and miraculous healings.' Cancer cured after visiting Lourdes.

---

[82] *Hedwig and the Angry Inch.*

They wear sweaters and low ponytails. They all sound the same when they talk. "Garrett's going through a lot of turmoil. But I feel we're moving closer together in our spiritual life. I just feel a lot of anxiety at this time of year. This time of life. I know I seek a lot of worldly gratification." Hangs head in shame. Shrouds shoulders with pride.

To amputate God is to make room for other things. Clean house. To worship not at church but at Church. At the temple of the body literally born again.

Eyes shining. Wound smiling. A reconciliation of the flesh.

On Saturday, two young men knock on **LORRIE**'s apartment door. They have pamphlets in their hands. Pocket-sized Bibles inscribed with the address of the rectory. The name and number of **FR. W**.

No one answers the door and so the men move on—but not before slipping beneath the door an invitation to church.

Through the steam of the hot tub, Lorrie and **BARTHOLOMEW** make meaningful eye contact. One knows what the other is thinking. Every moment is an opportunity to minister to those in need.

Lorrie turns her gaze to Big Tub—his incredible girth made more obvious by the lengths he's gone to hide it. "Hey," she says. Friendly. "Have you heard of Church?"

In her job at the museum, Lorrie was quick to learn the word-processing software adopted by the state. She can type nearly as fast as the thoughts form in her head. Nimble yet and young—raised in the age of technology—her fingers fly across the keys and she rarely makes mistakes. Lorrie grasps grammar and syntax like pencils: firmly. Deftly.

When she writes outside her job, however, she uses pencils, vomiting words from mind through graphite gullet in bold lines and dashed periods. The neat and slanting strokes of hard consonants. Vowels dripping their jellied contents like so much headcheese.

After Lorrie joins the Church, she officially becomes Captain Hook's left-hand woman (his missing arm—she holds onto the hook when they walk out in public). Assumes the role of sexton. She is recording a history in the making. A story of people-in-making, who for all their reticence continue to show up in pained, and panicked, and pleasure-seeking, peace-hungry droves. Bartholomew blessing them with the sign of the scalpel. Lorrie writes and she documents and in the writing finds a satisfaction that cures her own desire to disappear piece-by-piece. Finger by toe by lingering, unloved limb.

That day on the table, when she saved little Lorrie? In hugging herself to herself, Lorrie found a kind of wholeness that felt more real than the funeral they ultimately held for her severed tonsils—those shrunken, unnecessary, and already-forgotten parts of herself. Like all the little kids we once were.

She reads Steve Tomasula's *Vas* and Maggie Nelson's *The Argonauts* and, inspired, pieces together this book about what it means to be able-bodied and not want that body.

In the process, she learns to suture together again that

which, once sundered, would normally and had before left a hole. A stump. A new thing entirely. And to find joy working alongside Bartholomew, in the performances he creates, the freedom he engenders, and the story they are writing together.

Illustration No. 74:
I piglet nothing.

ODYSSEIA is invited to produce three more shows for museums in the U.S. after the success of her Civil War showing. Rumors breed like viruses and infect the internet. She becomes known in limited but international circles for her eccentricity as well as her art. The "reincarnated Dr. Braker." The limbless lesbian knockout. And her Cherokee shaman partner! They're like Ellen and Portia in all the best ways: beautiful; generous; graceful dancers. Odysseia starts cutting Monica's hair with her feet to save her a trip to the salon. Odysseia is very good with scissors.

On **FOREST**'s 20th birthday, he announces he's bringing another friend to dinner, and this time **TRICE** and **VICKI** know he means a girl. The boy's been in love for the last year. Her name is **ANNA**.

Things are serious.

Things are serious with Trice and Vicki, too. Despite the gulf of time, they've found a way to hold one another in ways that feel protective and not restrictive. They breathe the same air and know that love is a mathematical factor that multiplies.

Years later, some kids will stumble across **GEORGE**'s sun-bleached skeleton, his skin and clothes faded.pecked. blown away 'til nothing remains but bones. Scattered slightly—as though the body had been torn apart. Capped at one external acoustic meatus by a weather-matted clump of brown beaver fur.

Over the course of seven months, **DON** transforms into the father figure that **CARLOS** never had. The boy trusts the man and the man depends on the boy to do his bidding, promptly and without question every time. The warm-up tasks are tests. Behead the squawking chicken. Sterilize the goat where it stands: one snip. *When I prop my leg like an offering on the log—*

On Friday, Don prepares the third horse stall from the end. He mucks then sweeps out every piece of straw, every corner pile of straw dust. He adds soap to the power washer and sprays a heavy-duty detergent down the walls. It pools on then floods the concrete foundation. Soap bubbles pile up. *Pop.* Don uses a brand new push broom to squeegee the water out of the stall. He works methodically. He only takes his eyes off Carlos to make sure he's missed nothing.

CAPTAIN HOOK never charges for his services, so the congregation establishes a trust in the name of Mantid Labs. They make deposits like tithes, in amounts as preposterous as they are able. For how does one price the value of a life made complete for the very first time?

With the money, Mantid Labs develops even more powerful and ever more controlled explosives, and Bartholomew patents none of them. Because the technology, if used for ill, would undoubtedly destroy the world. And the point is to save mankind.

No one, including **ELIOT** himself, films the surgical removal of his penis. He does not, like **ODYSESSIA**, become a blip of an internet sensation: fodder for frat boys to crow over and dare new initiates at future hazings. But he'll replay the scene in his own mind for the rest of his life.

As the Church continues to grow, a committee forms to monitor the membership. By unanimous decision, they vote to canonize Eliot as the order's first saint.

A choking is also a staunching. When the last scab peels: new body.

1 And it came to pass in those days, that there went out a decree from **DON** to **CARLOS**, that two more limbs should be axed.

2 (And this axing was first conceived when Rauner was governor of Illinois.)

3 And Don went to be axed, into his own barn.

4 And Carlos also went up from his neighborhood, out of the city of Springfield, into the country, unto the barn of Don, which is called the shucking grounds; (because he was the grower and harvester of corn.)

5 To axe Don, his father figure-employer, being great with loyalty and desire.

6 And so it was, that, while they were there, the hours were accomplished that Don should be delivered.

7 And he brought forth his lastborn legs, and swaddling each upper thigh with a tourniquet, presented the limbs to Carlos. When Carlos had severed both legs, he laid Don in a manger; because there would no longer be room for him in **PETUNIA**'s bed.

8 And the boy who had shepherded Don into being, kept watch over his flock all night.

9 And, lo, they importuned Saint Anthony of Padua, patron saint of lost things (including limbs) and the glory of the Lord shone round about them.

10 And Anthony said unto them, *Behold, I bring you good tidings of great joy, which shall be to all people.*

11 *For unto all is re-born this day in the city of Springfield the Saviour of all elective amputees, which is Don.*

12 *And this shall be a sign unto them; they shall find the triple yet wrapped in matching tourniquets, lying in a manger.*

13 And suddenly there was with Saint Anthony a multitude of the heavenly host praising Don, and saying,

14 *Glory to Don in the highest, and on earth peace, good will toward humankind.*

15 And in Don's blood loss-induced delirium, he saw Petunia looking young as fresh as the day he married her, and his now-deceased parents as he remembered them from childhood, and all the men and women of the veterans' support group, all those boys with whom he'd once played at war.

16 And everyone looked on with shining eyes, applauding.

17 And when they had seen him, they made known abroad the saying which was told them concerning this man reborn as humble child.

18 And all they that heard it wondered at those things which were told them by witnesses.

19 And Carlos pondered those things in his heart, the Good Shepherd,

20 and then he walked slowly home.

21 And when eight days were accomplished and Petunia finally returned home from visiting her sister,

22 she went to the barn for to seek out her husband;

23 and opening the barn doors

24 a pair of pigeons fluttered out from the rafters.

25 And, behold, there was a man in a feed trough, whose name was Don; and while he was surely dead, he looked at peace, having received all the consolation of Israel: the Holy Ghost fed upon him.

28 Then shooing away the goat and taking Don up in her arms, Petunia blessed God, and said,

29 *Lord, now lettest thou thy servant depart in peace, according to thy word:*

30 *Yea, a sword shall pierce through my own soul also*

37 And Petunia became a widow of about fourscore and four years, who departed not from the farmhouse again, but served God with fastings and prayers and pie night and day.

"*Saint Anthony, please come around, there's something lost that must be found.*"

ACKNOWLEDGMENTS

Headcheese began life on Tumblr—an assorted collection of headlines, artwork, and broken bits of stories. To the early readers who offered their feedback and encouragement—Brandon Bross, Alexander Smith, Melissa Myers, Leo Rubinkowski—your support meant everything.

Chris Panatier: I had long admired your drawings from afar when I proposed this collaboration. You so graciously and enthusiastically dove right in. Let me know how I can repay you.

Nic Massie: We dated less than a month, but long enough for me to learn the story behind your missing leg … planting the seeds of the thousand questions that became this book.

Trice Johnson: your knowledge of prosthetics informed *Headcheese*. The prosthetics you design restore dignity to countless lives. Thank you for asking me to dance at The Absinthe House.

Phil Korsh: you were my only beta reader to follow through on the assignment. Our early meeting at Starbucks before Weeknight Wordsmiths one Monday night stood to make or break my resolve—and you convinced me that *Headcheese* was an idea worth pursuing. I've already promised the rest of the Wordsmiths bit parts in the movie version.

Keith Abbott: I hated your class at Naropa, but you made me prove to myself that I could write a novel. And here we are.

Cinestate, y'all are rad. Jess, Natasha, Preston, Dallas, Ashley, and Clay: I knew that *Headcheese* could be better, and gentle midwives all, you coaxed it from my heart.

Thank you.

CINESTATE.COM
@CINESTATEMENT
DALLAS, TX

CPSIA information can be obtained
at www.ICGtesting.com
Printed in the USA
LVHW032005131118
596997LV00008B/10